Praise for Mari Carr & Jayne Rylon's *Winter's Thaw*

"A cold Wyoming winter, a hot, sexy cowboy, and Sienna's sexual education will warm readers up in a hurry. [...] *Winter's Thaw* doesn't disappoint."

~ *Library Journal*

"From a scary overprotective dad to a rodeo mad younger brother, *Winter's Thaw* is more than just a love story. This is a story about a family; its ups and downs and everything in between."

~ *Night Owl Reviews*

"As always, the dynamic duo of Mari Carr and Jayne Rylon, have given the readers another wonderful series."

~ *Long and Short Reviews*

"Try this sizzling story and be inspired to live a little."

~ *Fresh Fiction*

"Having very much enjoyed the Compass Brothers series, I was delighted to find that *Winter's Thaw* contained the same humor, emotion and strong family connection, along with large doses of smoking hot love scenes."

~ *Romance Junkies*

Look for these titles by
Mari Carr

Now Available:

Because of You
Because You Love Me
Because It's True

Black & White
Erotic Research
Tequila Truth
Rough Cut
Happy Hour
Power Play
Slam Dunk

Second Chances
Fix You
Full Moon
Status Update

Compass Brothers

(Written with Jayne Rylon)
Northern Exposure
Southern Comfort
Eastern Ambitions
Western Ties

Compass Girls
(Written with Jayne Rylon)
Winter's Thaw
Hope Springs
Sizzlin' Summer

Print Collections
Learning Curves
Dangerous Curves
Love's Compass
Wicked Curves
Just Because

Look for these titles by Jayne Rylon

Now Available:

Nice and Naughty
Where There's Smoke

Men In Blue
Night is Darkest
Razor's Edge
Mistress's Master
Spread Your Wings

Powertools
Kate's Crew
Morgan's Surprise
Kayla's Gifts
Devon's Pair
Nailed to the Wall
Hammer It Home

Play Doctor
Dream Machine
Healing Touch

Compass Brothers
(Written with Mari Carr)
Northern Exposure
Southern Comfort
Eastern Ambitions
Western Ties

Compass Girls
(Written with Mari Carr)
Winter's Thaw
Hope Springs
Sizzlin' Summer

Hot Rods
King Cobra
Mustang Sally
Super Nova

Print Anthologies
Three's Company
Love's Compass
Powertools
Two to Tango
Love Under Construction

Winter's Thaw

Mari Carr & Jayne Rylon

*Julie,
I hope you find a love for every season!
Jayne Rylon*

SAMHAIN
PUBLISHING

Samhain Publishing, Ltd.
11821 Mason Montgomery Road, 4B
Cincinnati, OH 45249
www.samhainpublishing.com

Winter's Thaw
Copyright © 2014 by Mari Carr & Jayne Rylon
Print ISBN: 978-1-61921-685-3
Digital ISBN: 978-1-61921-333-3

Editing by Amy Sherwood
Cover by Valerie Tibbs

This book is a work of fiction. The names, characters, places, and incidents are products of the writer's imagination or have been used fictitiously and are not to be construed as real. Any resemblance to persons, living or dead, actual events, locale or organizations is entirely coincidental.

All Rights Are Reserved. No part of this book may be used or reproduced in any manner whatsoever without written permission, except in the case of brief quotations embodied in critical articles and reviews.

First Samhain Publishing, Ltd. electronic publication: February 2013
First Samhain Publishing, Ltd. print publication: February 2014

Dedication

This story is dedicated to the strong women in our lives—our grandmothers, Mary, Virginia, Gretchen and Ruth; our mothers, Linda and Susan; and to daughter Glen.

Prologue

"Shh. Quiet," Sienna Compton warned as she and her cousins snuck into her family's barn. It was nearly two a.m. on her sixteenth birthday. Sweet sixteen. At last.

Her cousins—and best friends—Jade, Sterling and Hope had planned a sleepover to celebrate with her. They'd piggy-piled into sleeping bags in Sienna's bedroom shortly after ten, chatting and giggling for hours. Her dad, Seth, had come in twice to tell them to quiet down.

After a couple hours of whispered conversations, the rest of the house fell silent. That was when Jade had climbed out of her sleeping bag, tiptoed to the door and listened for a moment before declaring the coast was clear.

When Sterling had asked what the heck it was clear for, Jade had refused to answer, picking up her backpack and telling them to follow her. On their way out, they'd detoured through the kitchen so Jade could grab a saltshaker and oranges.

As they reached the hayloft, Sienna grabbed a camp lantern from the supply room and they each took a turn climbing the ladder. Once they reached the top, Sienna turned on the lamp. It cast the area in an eerie, dim light. They sat in a small circle facing each other as Jade produced a bottle of tequila from her bag.

Hope's eyes went wide. "Where did you get that?"

"I smuggled it out of my parents' liquor cabinet."

Sterling shook her head in disbelief. "Uncle Sawyer is going to ground you until you're forty-seven."

Jade shrugged, unconcerned. "It's Sienna's sixteenth birthday. We need to do something special."

"The cake I baked for her wasn't enough?" Hope asked.

Sienna reached over to touch her cousin's hand. "The cake was perfect. Chocolate is my favorite."

Jade rolled her eyes. "We always have cake on our birthdays. I thought tonight called for something different. The Mothers always pull this out on special occasions to make a toast. Why shouldn't we do the same thing?"

Sienna grinned at Jade's nickname for their moms. The Mothers, as she and her cousins had taken to calling them, were a force unto themselves around Compass Ranch. Sienna was proud to come from such a long line of strong, self-confident women. Her mother, Jody, and aunts Leah, Lucy and Cindi, as well as her beloved grandmother, Vicky—Vivi to them—had raised her to believe in herself, always offering encouragement and unwavering support.

Sienna was part of the Compton heritage, a family whose name was synonymous with power and honor in Compton Pass. The town had been named after her gazillions-great grandfather, and it had grown quite a bit during the years since her granddaddy JD's death over fifteen years earlier. Though she'd never met JD, his legacy certainly lived on, and Sienna felt as though she had known him through the stories Vivi told her.

"I turned sixteen in May and you didn't steal tequila for me." Hope crossed her arms, appearing only slightly put out. Sienna knew her cousin was uncomfortable with the trouble they were risking with this escapade. While Sterling and Jade were the more rebellious of the foursome, she and Hope tended to walk a straighter, narrower line in terms of following the rules.

"I tried," Jade explained, "but you decided to have a big-ass Sweet Sixteen party at the community center with our whole family and half of Compton Pass. There wasn't anywhere to hide the damn bottle in that fancy dress I had to wear."

Hope's birthday party was still a bone of contention between the two girls. Jade resided squarely in the middle of tomboy camp. Wearing a dress to any event was akin to eating manure. Sienna recalled Aunt Leah telling the other Mothers about the battle she'd waged to get Jade to wear the simple green dress. Aunt Leah knew Jade well enough to buy her a dress without frills, but regardless of her efforts, Jade resisted putting it on. Jade had insisted she'd look just fine in her new jeans, but Aunt Leah had stuck to her guns.

"You were really pretty that night." Hope remained resolute in her choice of fancy attire for the party. "Half of the boys in our class looked like their eyes would pop out of their heads when you showed up."

"I think you're mistaking shock for interest. So, are we gabbing or are we drinking?" Jade pulled the cork out of the bottle of Patrón.

Sterling took a quick sniff, scowling. "Jesus. That smells terrible."

Jade wasn't deterred, picking up an orange and peeling it. "The salt and limes are supposed to take the burn off."

Sienna pointed out the obvious. "We don't have limes."

"Hence the oranges. I guess it's about the same. They're both juicy fruits. Personally, I think the orange might taste better. It's sweeter." Jade broke the orange slices apart and placed them on a napkin in the center of their circle.

Sterling began to fill the shot glasses. "Guess we should go ahead and see what the fuss is about, since Jade went to all this trouble."

Sienna didn't think Sterling was too bothered by the prospect of trying the shot. Of course, that was par for the course for Sterling. She was usually up for anything.

Sterling handed each girl a glass.

Sienna didn't even have to lift it to her nose to catch the overwhelming scent of alcohol. Jade licked her hand, sprinkled salt on it and then passed the shaker around, gesturing for them to do the same.

"So it's salt, shot and orange," Jade instructed, though none of them needed the tutorial. The Mothers had been following this same birthday tradition for as long as the girls had been alive.

"Aren't we supposed to propose a toast?" Hope asked as they lifted their glasses.

"I have one," Jade said. "Here's to all the boys whose hearts we're going to break this year. Poor suckers."

They drank the shots, each of them wincing as they sucked on the sweet oranges they hoped would kill the taste.

"That's awful," Hope declared, wrinkling her nose and covering her mouth. "Totally gross. Why would anyone drink that?"

Sterling didn't bother to respond. Instead, she studied Jade's face. "Whose heart are you planning to break? I thought you had the hots for Evan. And I get the feeling he likes you too. You already sick of him?"

Jade shook her head. "I wasn't thinking of anyone in particular. We're all going to be sixteen soon. Hope and Sienna are already there, and you and I are celebrating our birthdays in January. Let's face it. None of us is going to meet *the one* for a damn long time—if ever. In the meantime, I plan to be the dumper, not the dumpee. There's no way you'll catch me crying for weeks over a boy like Jenna Garber did when Russ Philpott broke up with her."

"Jenna was ridiculous," Sterling agreed.

Hope, ever the compassionate one, chimed in. "Russ was her first love. And he immediately started going out with her best friend. That's pretty harsh."

"This," Jade explained, "is why I'm always going to make sure I throw the first punch. No boy is ever going to get close enough to break my heart."

Sienna shook her head. "I don't think that's a very smart way to live your life. And you're wrong about us being too young to realize if someone's the one. Look at me and Josh. We've been together for nearly four months, and he's totally awesome. There's no way I'm leaving him. We're going to go to the same college, then come back here to live in Compton Pass. We want the same things. That's why we're so perfect together. I don't plan on breaking his heart and he won't break mine."

"How can you plan forever with a guy you've never gone past second base with?" Jade asked. "Uncle Seth's never even let you go on a car date alone with Josh."

"That's because I was only fifteen. Now that I'm sixteen and I can get my driver's license, Dad said I can go out with him. And even if we haven't gone on a real date, that doesn't mean we haven't kissed. A lot."

Jade rolled her eyes. "Kissing. Big deal."

"Josh respects me. He said we could wait until I'm ready. Besides, unless I missed the memo, you haven't even walked up to the plate with Evan. You're both still in that middle school, arm-punching phase."

Jade narrowed her eyes. "Ha ha. I told you. I'm not settling for the first guy to glance my way. Or even the second or third or—"

"We get the picture." Hope, ever the peacemaker, picked up another orange slice and tried to steer the conversation to safer waters. "You and Josh are great together, Sienna. I wish I could meet a guy—or two—like him."

Sienna grinned. Rather than two parents, Hope had three. Uncle Silas and Uncle Colby were both married to Hope's mother, Lucy. While Sienna realized there were folks around town who thought the union was weird and looked down on it, Sienna thought it was beautiful. She knew Hope couldn't see it as anything but natural and would be open to the same type of relationship.

Sterling's view of relationships was harder to put a finger on. Sterling wasn't quite the romantic Sienna and Hope were, nor was her view of relationships quite as jaded as...well, Jade's. In most things, Sterling marched to the beat of her own drummer, which made her nearly impossible for Sienna to read.

"I think we're too young to worry about any of this." Sterling poured another round. "This stuff isn't so bad. I'm feeling sort of warm and fuzzy inside. Should we try another one?"

Sienna was surprised when Jade and Hope both agreed. Never one to be left out, she accepted the salt and the glass again.

Once again, Jade proposed the toast. "Here's to the Compass Girls, the craziest cousins west of the Mississippi."

They laughed as they drank, and this time, no one disagreed.

Chapter One

Six years later...

Sienna stepped out onto the front porch of her family's house and pulled her jacket more tightly against her. It was damn chilly for mid-October. If the cool autumn was an indicator, she'd guess they were in for a long, frosty winter. Typically she enjoyed the return of cold air, hot chocolate, skiing and snowy mornings, but this year, she wasn't looking forward to any of it.

Her distaste for the season probably had to do with the fact she'd be spending most of the winter without Josh. The idea of enduring the icy months without him was depressing. For years, it had been their favorite season as they celebrated the holidays together with their families, took weekend ski trips to Snowy Range or just cuddled in front of the fireplace at the ranch.

Unfortunately, she was home alone while Josh was still away at college. To add insult to injury, he'd begun dropping hints in his past few emails that he'd been invited to spend Christmas with his college roommates in Florida. He hadn't come out and said he was accepting, but she definitely got the sense he was feeling her out and trying to get her consent.

The idea of spending the holidays without Josh wasn't sitting well with her. As a result, she'd been walking around the past few weeks like a bear with a thorn in her paw, snapping and attacking her family with very little provocation. She was turning into a bitch and hating herself for it.

"What on Earth are you doing standing out here? It's cold as a tomb today."

Sienna turned as Vivi tugged a shawl over her shoulders and joined her on the porch. "Dad just called from the road. Said he and the boys were almost home. Apparently, they've got a surprise."

Her dad and younger brothers, Doug and James, had driven to Casper a few days earlier to attend a trade show featuring rodeo equipment. Her brothers—hell, her entire family—were rodeo-mad. Not that she blamed them. Doug and James were extremely talented riders who excelled in nearly every competition. She'd even participated in the sport when she was in high school. For three years running, she'd been the top barrel racer in her division.

"Wonder what they could be bringing." Vivi's gaze drifted down the long stretch of road that would lead the guys home from the highway. "You suppose they bought another horse?"

Sienna rolled her eyes. Her father, Seth, had been increasing their stable quite a bit the past few months, taking his interest in horse breeding out of the hobby range and turning it into a full-fledged career. "I wouldn't consider that very shocking. Seems like lately all they do is come home with new horses. Although I don't know how they'd get it here from Casper. They didn't take a trailer with them."

"Seth always was crazy about horses. Lord knows this ranch is big enough to support this new venture of his. Sam seems to think we'll turn a pretty fair profit from the fine horseflesh Seth's hoping to breed."

Sienna leaned against the railing. "Yeah, but between the

horses, the other ranch chores and the time Dad spends working with the boys on their rodeo skills, Mom seems to think he's wearing himself a bit thin."

"Jody has said the same thing to me. She's trying to encourage him to hire more help, but that boy can be stubborn as a mule sometimes."

Sienna grinned at her grandmother calling her nearly fifty-year-old father a boy. In Vivi's eyes, her beloved sons would always be her boys. "Well, so can Mom. It might be fun to see who wins this fight."

Vivi moved closer. Sienna suspected it was to share body heat as the breeze picked up. She knew she should suggest they go inside, but Sienna needed the fresh air. It helped clear her rather disconcerting thoughts.

"It will be little surprise to either of us who wins, Sienna. Seth would move heaven and earth to make your mom happy."

Sienna's smile dimmed a bit. She recognized the truth behind her grandmother's words and it reminded her of why she'd come outside in the first place.

Josh.

She used to believe they were soul mates, destined to share the same enduring love Sienna witnessed every day between her parents. Now, she was starting to question those feelings.

"What's wrong, See?"

Sienna had never been able to hide anything from Vivi. "Just missing Josh."

Vivi sighed. "That boy has some growing up to do."

Sienna shrugged, though she certainly agreed. "Maybe he does. Did I tell you he's hinting around about possibly going to Florida with his roommates from college over the holidays?"

Her grandmother's scowl told her she wasn't any happier

with Josh's desire to miss a Compton Pass Christmas than Sienna was. Of course, if it had just been the trip, maybe Sienna could have understood, but lately, Josh was doing a lot of things she couldn't wrap her head around.

"That young man needs to get his head out of his ass. Pardon my language." Oh yeah. Vivi was annoyed. She rarely cursed.

Strangely, her grandmother's response made Sienna feel less guilty about her own anger. "I agree with you. I can't figure him out these days."

Since they were fifteen years old, she and Josh had walked the same path, hand in hand. They'd chosen to attend the same university after graduating from high school and their master plan had never wavered. She would become a nurse, he a teacher. They'd come home to Compton Pass, get married and live happily ever after. Sienna was still committed to that dream.

As for Josh…

Vivi tightened her grip on her shawl when another gust of wind blew over them. "I was surprised when he changed his major. Thought he was determined to be a teacher."

"So did I. I'm sure his parents are thrilled he's chosen to study business so that he'll be better prepared to take over the store when they retire, but I think they would have preferred he made that decision before they spent so much money on an education he won't be using."

Josh's family owned and operated the local hardware store. As an only child, Josh stood to inherit the prosperous business. For most of his life, Josh had insisted he had no desire to run the store. Sienna wasn't sure what had happened to change his mind. He'd simply stood up after Thanksgiving dinner last year and announced he was switching his major and that his four-year college plan would now take five.

Sienna had been as shocked as his parents and hurt that he'd made the decision without discussing it with her first. Not that she would have tried to talk him out of it. She'd never ask him to pursue a career if it wasn't something that would make him happy. But weren't they supposed to be partners? They'd mapped out their futures together. So why did Josh take a detour without her?

"I've been worried about you, See. I know you miss Josh, but you're still young. There's no reason why your life should be put on hold while you wait for that boy to come home. Why don't you take Jade up on her offer the next time she invites you for a girls' night out?"

Sienna made a pained face. "Jade's idea of fun is a million miles away from mine, Vivi. If she was interested in dinner and a movie or shopping or something like that, I'd be there. For her, girls' night out involves crowded bars, loud music and pool tables. I'm not in the mood to spend an evening fending off a bunch of drunk rednecks, while trying to keep Jade from getting into a fight with whoever is stupid enough to cross her path."

Vivi chuckled. "I suppose you're right. That girl has a wild streak a mile wide. Gonna take a pretty special man to love her without breaking her spirit."

"Personally, I think she could do with a bit less of that damn spirit."

Vivi shook her head. "No. Jade's just fine the way she is." Vivi seemed to be the only Compton who didn't see anything wrong with Jade's rebelliousness, though she had to admit there were times when Sienna wished she was more like her carefree cousin. Jade lived in the moment, never thinking much beyond what the next five minutes would bring. Sienna had never mastered that concept."

"In fact," Vivi continued, "I think all my granddaughters have grown up to become amazing young women."

Sienna smiled at her grandmother's compliment, grasping Vivi's hand and squeezing it gently. "Thanks."

She glanced down the road at the sound of tires on gravel. She spotted her father's truck. "Looks like the guys are home."

Vivi followed her glance, her brow creasing. "Why did all three of them go into town again?"

Sienna paused, studying her grandmother's face. "They weren't in town, Vivi. They went to a trade show in Casper. Remember?"

"Oh. That's right." Lately, Vivi's sharp-as-a-tack mind seemed to wander more. While Vivi's memories were still there, Sienna noticed her grandmother found it more difficult to recall day-to-day happenings or the names of new ranch hands or where she left her glasses. Sienna attributed the slight lapses to age. After all, Vivi was over seventy.

"What's that coming up behind Seth's truck?"

Sienna turned at Vivi's question and spotted an RV that was at least two decades past its prime following her father's vehicle. "Holy crap. Do you think Dad bought that eyesore? Mom will kill him."

Vivi chuckled. "I'm surprised it still runs."

Mom joined them on the front porch. "What the hell is that?"

Sienna grinned. "We have no idea, but at least it's not a horse."

Mom turned and gave her a heavy sigh. "I'd prefer a horse. At least they're nice to look at. Besides, who's driving that thing?"

Sienna glanced at her dad's truck. There in the cab sat her father and both of her brothers, grinning like fools. Her mother sometimes despaired over exactly how much Doug and James were like their father. Said she had a hard enough time keeping Seth in line. Now that he'd acquired two mini-me's, the task had become impossible. Sienna knew the complaint was said with love. Despite the definite streak of stubbornness that ran through the male Comptons, they were compassionate and dedicated to their family and the land. Add to that their undeniable charm and wit and it made for a pretty irresistible combination.

Dad climbed out of the truck, his arms spread wide. Mom's annoyance over the camper obviously wasn't long lasting. She dashed off the stairs and straight into her husband's arms. Dad wrapped her mom in an embrace that usually warmed Sienna's heart. Today, though, it reminded her of her loneliness for Josh, and a lump formed in her throat.

Her brothers grabbed their backpacks out of the truck cab and headed toward the stairs. "Hey, See. Hiya, Vivi," Doug said as he approached them. "You missed a helluva show."

Vivi put her hands on her hips. "What have I told you about that cursing, Douglas Compton?"

"Aw dammit, Vivi, I'm a grown man. All men cuss."

Sienna fought to hide her smile. Her baby brother, Doug, had just turned eleven and he was too precocious for his own good. She suspected his rush to grow up stemmed from the fact he idolized his older brother, James. At fifteen, James had everything Doug wanted: a learner's permit, a girlfriend and—according to Doug—really cool hair.

Dad came up behind his son. "Doug, what was I saying to you not ten minutes ago in that truck?"

Doug's shoulders flew up guiltily. Obviously, he was

surprised he'd been caught by Dad. "Sorry, Sienna. Sorry, Vivi."

Sienna, unable to fight it, let her grin show. She was glad to have her dad and brothers home. Even though they'd only been gone a few days, the ranch was always too quiet without them. They brought life to the place. Especially Doug.

It wasn't until her father stepped closer to the porch that Sienna realized they weren't alone. Her breath caught when she spotted the stranger who was standing in their midst and she mouthed a silent *whoa*.

Dad turned toward him. "Jody, I'd like you to meet Daniel Lennon."

Mom extended her hand and the handsome cowboy shook it.

"Pleasure to meet you, ma'am."

"Likewise," her mother said with a friendly smile.

Seth gestured to where she and Vivi stood. "And these two lovely ladies are my mother, Vicky, and my daughter, Sienna."

Daniel tipped his hat in a courteous gesture toward Vivi, then his coal-black gaze met Sienna's. He was the most handsome man Sienna had ever seen. Even as she thought it, she felt guilty for comparing Daniel's sexy-as-sin five-o'clock shadow to Josh's baby-soft cheeks.

"Sienna," Daniel said softly. It felt as if he was trying the name on for style. She'd actually never cared for her name. At least not until that moment. She'd often complained about being named after a crayon. And not even one of the pretty colors. A brown one.

However, the way Daniel said it, slowly, almost like a caress, made her think of sex and sweaty sheets and naughty, *naughty* things. Sienna blinked rapidly and forced herself to glance away from the good-looking cowboy. She was standing next to her grandmother, for God's sake, and imagining doing all sorts of wicked things with a man she'd only just met.

Her horniness was Josh's fault. He'd headed back to the university at the end of August and hadn't bothered to make even a quick weekend trip home since then. They'd have to make up for lost time over Thanksgiving.

"What brings you to Compass Ranch, Daniel?" Leave it to Vivi to cut to the chase and ask the question on the tip of every woman's tongue.

"I hired him," Dad replied. "He's going to help me start my horse breeding business. I called Sam last night and we decided the time was right to diversify a bit. Silas and Colby are more than capable of handing the cattle side of things. Sam and I are interested in seeing if we can make a real go of the horses—more than just the tinkering I've been doing the past few months."

Mom smiled, wrapping her arm around Dad's waist. "I think that's a wonderful idea. So you're familiar with horse breeding, Daniel?"

Daniel nodded. "Yes, ma'am. I grew up on a farm in Loudoun County, Virginia. I was working with the horses alongside my dad from the time I could walk." Sienna tried to ignore the effect Daniel's slight southern twang was having on her more private parts. Better to blame her suddenly taut nipples on the cool October breeze.

"How did a Virginia boy end up all the way over here in Wyoming?" Vivi asked.

Doug answered for him, too excited about the news he had to share. "The rodeo. Daniel was a rodeo star and he's gonna teach me and James all the tricks. He rode the bulls, Vivi. Loads of times. He's retired now, though." Rodeo riders were Doug's superheroes. While most eleven-year-olds wished they could be Batman or Superman, Doug had always insisted he would be a bull rider. Sienna, like her mother, prayed it was a dream that would pass as he grew older. She hated the thought of her baby brother ever doing anything so dangerous.

Now that her father had brought this man here, it was going to be even more difficult to discourage Doug's youthful aspirations.

Daniel was still staring at her. His gaze was almost unnerving. No one had ever studied her with such blatant interest. *Sexual* interest.

Time to nip things in the bud. She had enough on her plate without dealing with some horny ranch hand. "A bull rider, huh? You seem awfully young to be retired. Were you not very good at it?"

Dad blinked, surprise and confusion written on his face at her rudeness. Her tone sounded hostile even to her own ears.

"Sienna," Dad started, but Daniel didn't appear to take offense.

"I was injured pretty badly during my last ride. It put a quick end to my future with the rodeo."

Sienna felt like dirt. God dammit. What was wrong with her? She bit her lower lip. "I'm sorry."

Daniel grinned. "Why? You weren't the bull. Anyway, I packed up my trailer and decided to try my hand at being a salesman for a rodeo equipment company. Met your dad at the trade show and he took mercy on me. Apparently, I suck at sales."

Dad chuckled and patted Daniel on the back in a friendly gesture. Sienna was curious about how this man had earned her father's fondness in just a few days. "The man is too damn honest. He wasn't content with just telling me what was good about the items he was peddling. He also felt compelled to explain what was wrong with them."

James piped up. "He told us how the strap on one of the saddles broke and cost him a rodeo championship."

"I can see how that might have impacted sales," Mom said, laughing.

"Anyway, we invited him to join us for lunch. One thing led to another and I realized that with his knowledge of horse breeding, he would be an asset to Compass Ranch."

"And don't forget he's going to teach us how to be real rodeo cowboys," Doug added, stressing what was clearly the most important part of Daniel's new duties on the ranch.

Daniel reached over and messed up Doug's hair. "I'm only going to teach you if you promise to stop cussing in front of ladies. Cowboys are always gentlemen."

Doug nodded his consent. Sienna suspected her little brother would also promise Daniel the moon on a silver platter and the dirty magazine he had hidden under his bed if it meant he'd get his lessons.

Dad pointed to the rickety RV. "And better yet, Daniel comes to us with his own lodging. Sienna, why don't you help him pick out a nice spot to set up camp while the boys and I unpack the truck? Unfortunately, not all the salespeople at the trade show were bad at their jobs. I bought way too much."

Mom grinned. "I'll remember that the next time I go shopping with Cindi, Leah and Lucy."

Vivi walked to the front door. "I've got a big pot of spaghetti sauce simmering on the stove. I hope you'll join us for dinner, Daniel."

Daniel gave her grandmother a smile that was far too charming, and Sienna felt the effects of it in places she didn't care to acknowledge. "Thank you, Mrs. Compton. Spaghetti sounds real good."

"Call me Vicky. I think you'll find we're not big on formalities here at the ranch."

Daniel touched the brim of his hat again, the old-fashioned gesture touching...and sexy. "Thank you, Vicky."

Sienna took a deep breath. Dammit. She wouldn't be feeling so hot and bothered if Josh had just stuck to the plan. She'd never abstained for so long. Sex was one of the best perks of a steady boyfriend, as far as she was concerned.

Daniel waited for her to descend the stairs and then led her to his RV. Opening the passenger door, he gestured for her to climb in. "Welcome to my palace, Sienna."

His voice was pure mischief. Sienna could tell by the perceptive look in his eyes he knew she wasn't as immune to his charms as she wished. No doubt Daniel was a ladies' man, used to having his pick of the buckle bunnies. Well, he was going to be disappointed if he expected her to fall all over herself trying to turn his head.

She claimed her seat without giving him a sideways glance. Instead, she stared through the dirty windshield, wondering how much space she could put between his rusty RV and the house, the stables, her.

Daniel climbed behind the wheel and started the engine. "Your dad said there are plenty of side paths where I can park this monster without being in the way."

Compass Ranch was a massive property. It not only supported the main house, where she lived with her family and Vivi, but also held homes for Uncle Silas and Uncle Sam and their families. The only Compton brother who didn't live on the property was Uncle Sawyer, who'd opted for a home in town, so he could be close to the police department where he worked as Sheriff.

Sienna twisted in the seat to study the rest of the RV. For its inauspicious outer appearance, she had to admit the inside appeared neat and downright cozy. "You really live in here?"

He followed the driveway, passing the main house and stable. "I spent several years on the road with the rodeo. For the first few months, I either pitched a tent or slept in my truck. That got old pretty quick. Decided a house on wheels was a necessity. I got lucky. I was able to pick this beauty up real cheap and she offers a comfortable bed and place to kick up my feet after a long day."

Sienna snorted at the word *beauty*. Daniel grinned. He was obviously aware of the less than attractive state of his so-called *perfect* home. He winked at her.

Daniel was an easygoing, nice guy. She felt guilty about her earlier rudeness. "I really am sorry to hear you were hurt so badly. How long ago did it happen?"

Daniel considered her question. "Hmm. Let me see. Almost a year ago to the day. Guess I'm celebrating an anniversary of sorts. I spent six months recuperating and then three more in rehab. I'd only been doing the sales job a few months. Thankfully, I met your dad. He's a great guy. Pretty sure he saved me from a life of poverty. There was no way in hell I was gonna make ends meet as a salesman."

She smiled, trying to make amends for their rough beginning. "I'm glad you took him up on his offer. He's been planning to get this new business off the ground for a while now. Between tinkering with the horse breeding and running my brothers all over God's creation for rodeo events, he was running out of hours in the day to do everything he wanted to." She pointed to smaller path off the main road. "Turn here. I think this is a good area."

They were quiet as Daniel maneuvered the RV over the

rutty lane.

"There's a turnaround spot on the right that might be a nice place for you to park this monstrosity. No one uses this lane anymore. It used to lead to a storage shed that was abandoned back during my Granddaddy JD's day. The actual building fell down a few years ago during a bad storm and my Uncle Colby had the remains hauled off."

Daniel backed the RV into the spot she indicated, then turned off the vehicle. He glanced around at their surroundings. "It's nice back here. Private, but not too far away from the stable or main house." He looked at her. "Thanks for your help, Sienna."

She licked her lips nervously, suddenly realizing how alone they were in the shelter of the woods. His face was the epitome of harmlessness, but there was something in his eyes that lured her, tempted her.

"Well," she said too loudly, "I guess I'll head back to the house and let you settle in."

"That's the beauty of an RV. Once you're parked, you're pretty much settled. I just have to throw some wheel chocks under the tires, expand the slide outs and voila—home sweet home. Want a tour?"

She did...and she didn't. Daniel had been nothing but friendly to her. Regardless, he left her unsettled. She'd never felt an attraction to any man except Josh. Ever. Her cousins told her that was a sad commentary for her life, but Sienna stood by her assertion that she'd been lucky, meeting her true love at fifteen.

She still felt that way. Sort of.

Daniel took her silence as acquiescence and rose, leaving the driver's seat and walking into the living room area. "I'm sure it seems small now, but that wall behind the couch slides out.

Once I've got the whole thing opened up, it's actually bigger than you might expect."

She'd spent nearly an entire summer in a similar RV with her family one year when her mother insisted it was time they saw more of the world than Wyoming. They'd driven to Texas in a borrowed RV to visit Granddaddy Thomas, then taken a meandering tour through Arizona, New Mexico, Nevada and several other states. Her parents had taken them to the Grand Canyon, the Hoover Dam, Mount Rushmore and Las Vegas.

By the end of the summer, Sienna had seen plenty of the country. She was also on the verge of killing her entire family after spending so much time confined with them in the small space. The experience had left her less than fond of RV'ing. She'd made a vow to herself that when she and Josh had kids, they'd travel the traditional way—in planes and hotels.

"It's very nice." Her tone must have betrayed her true thoughts.

Daniel chuckled. "Not much for hitting the open road and camping along the way, huh?"

She shrugged. "I like my vacations a little more organized."

"Organized how?"

Her answer was simple. "Plane tickets with definite departure and arrival times, hotel reservations and a detailed itinerary. Driving around with no definite idea of where you're going or when you'll get there is insanity."

Daniel shook his head. "Haven't you ever heard the expression *It's the journey, not the destination?*"

"No doubt that was penned by someone who couldn't be bothered to go online and book a room."

Daniel didn't respond. Instead, he simply studied her face. When she began to feel uncomfortable under his scrutiny, she turned and pretended to be fascinated by his kitchen. "You cook a lot?"

He shook his head. "I have enough skill not to starve. Mainly live on soup and sandwiches. Oh, and I can whip up a mean breakfast—scrambled eggs and bacon."

"Well, it sounds like Vivi is saving you from a light dinner tonight. Her homemade spaghetti sauce is to die for."

"Vivi?"

"Vicky, my grandmother. My cousin, Hope, dubbed her Vivi when she was two years old. She tried to say Vicky, but Vivi was all she could manage. There were three more of us learning to talk at about the same time, so the name stuck."

"Seth told me a bit about your family. Sounds like there are a lot of Comptons living on Compass Ranch."

She smiled. Talking about her family was never a hardship. She adored each and every cousin, aunt and uncle. "There are. I'm sure you'll meet most of them tomorrow morning. All of my uncles except Sawyer work on the ranch. My aunt Cindi is the bookkeeper. My mom and Vivi take care of the main house and keeping the ranch hands fed."

"Must be nice to have such a big family around all the time."

"It is. I love living here. What about your family?"

"Just me and my parents. I had an older brother, but he was killed in a motorcycle accident when he was eighteen."

Sienna reached out before she could think better of it. She lightly touched his arm. "I'm so sorry. That's terrible."

Daniel glanced down at her hand. Rather than shrug it off, he covered it with his. His face appeared relaxed, but his eyes had darkened with the memory. "It was. Took me a long time to come to terms with it. Such a huge waste. He was a great brother—smart and funny. Eventually I found a way to move on."

"How?" she asked.

"I think about him every day. I remember that life's short. There aren't any guaranteed tomorrows, so it's a smart idea to take advantage of today."

His response annoyed her, and her fingers dropped from his arm. "That's rather shortsighted, wouldn't you say?"

"What?"

Sienna wasn't sure what had triggered the damn temper she was helpless to keep contained lately, but she found herself unleashing far too much anger on this stranger. "I guess you've never given a thought to the consequences of your actions and how they might affect others. God, your poor mother must've died a million deaths when you told her you were joining the rodeo. She'd already lost one son and then you head off to do something reckless and dangerous too."

"My mother understood my love of the rodeo and wanted me to be happy. She supported my career choice."

Sienna shook her head. "I bet what she said and what she felt were two different things. It's pretty callous of you to think only of yourself without caring about what you're doing to the people who love you."

Daniel frowned. "I love my mother and I wouldn't do anything to hurt her. If you knew me better—hell, if you knew me at all—you'd understand that."

She sucked in a deep breath. What the hell was wrong with her? She was chastising a stranger for his choices in life. She was losing her mind these days. "I apologize. I didn't mean—"

"Who's hurting *you*, Sienna?"

She couldn't speak the real answer. She hadn't even

admitted it to herself, so she grasped a lie instead. It was easier. "No one. I'll see you at the house for dinner."

She stepped out of his trailer before he could question her further, but Daniel didn't take the hint.

"Hey, See," he called from the doorway.

She turned to face him, debating whether or not she should chastise him for using her family's nickname for her. It was too personal. Too close.

"You got a boyfriend?" he asked.

She nodded.

"Does he drive motorcycles? Ride with the circuit?"

She smirked, understanding full well where he was going with his questions. "No, he doesn't. He's away at college, studying business."

He graced her with that charming, deadly grin she'd seen earlier. "Serious boyfriend?"

She tilted her head. "Very serious. We're going to get married and buy a house in Compton Pass. He'll inherit his parents' hardware store while I work as a nurse and—God willing—we're going to have a couple kids."

He glanced at her left hand. She felt compelled to stuff it in her pocket so she wouldn't have to acknowledge his shrewd look that told her there was no ring on her finger yet. "So you got it all figured out, do you?"

She nodded, wishing he wouldn't give her that wicked look that made her think wholly inappropriate thoughts.

"Kind of reminds me of another saying."

"My, aren't you the king of quotations."

He didn't bother to acknowledge her snide comment. "A wise man once said the best laid plans often go astray. Seems to me your well-organized life could benefit from some shaking up."

"My life is just fine. And none of your damn business."

"Maybe. Maybe not." Daniel gave her a sexy, suggestive wink before turning and heading inside his trailer.

Sienna should confront him, blast him for being so forward, but the door slammed before she could form a proper retort.

She spun and headed back to the house, feeling furious and foolish. Daniel Lennon had a talent for twisting her words...and her insides into knots.

She didn't need this.

God, she *really* didn't need this.

Chapter Two

Daniel sat astride his horse and watched the clock as Doug ran a few drills to improve his barrel racing. He had been living on Compass Ranch for two weeks and for the first time in ages, he felt at home somewhere. The Compton family was, as his mother liked to say, good folk. They worked hard, played hard and, from what he could tell, they *fell* hard. He'd never met so many devoted, wholly in love couples in his life. After several years traveling the rodeo circuit, he'd seen one marriage after another crumble amongst the cowboys. So many, in fact, he'd sworn off commitment and sticky entanglements for a while. Living in Compton Pass had started to renew his faith in the institution, made him think that hitching himself to a pretty woman wouldn't be such a hardship.

"How was that?" Doug asked, riding alongside him.

Daniel checked the clock. "Not bad. You shaved about half a second off your time."

Doug's grin grew. The boy reminded Daniel of himself when he was younger. There was no denying Doug had been bitten by the rodeo bug. While James enjoyed the sport, for the older boy it was just a way to pass the time until graduation, and to impress girls. Doug, however, was constantly driven to learn, to improve.

Doug sidled closer. "You think you'll ever go back out on

the circuit?"

For a long time after his accident, Daniel had considered returning, despite the doctor's advice. He often dreamed he'd be the one to beat the odds, to come back stronger and better than before. Reality has a way of kicking you in the teeth. His arm wasn't—and wouldn't ever be—powerful enough to allow him to compete competitively.

He shook his head. "No. I'm afraid not."

Doug's young face reflected exactly how much he knew that loss must hurt. "Do you miss it?"

Daniel smiled sadly. "Yep. I sure do."

"Yeah. I would too. Bet you had a lot of girlfriends when you were riding the bulls."

Daniel swatted Doug playfully with his hat. "Is that the only reason you're practicing so hard? To get that cute little blonde thing I saw hanging out here yesterday to notice you?"

Doug blushed and shook his head emphatically. "Hell no. I don't like Denise. She's annoying."

"What did I say about your cussing?"

Doug glanced around. "There ain't any ladies here right now."

Daniel couldn't argue with the boy's logic. "You got me there."

"You got a girlfriend?" Doug asked.

"No." Daniel hadn't had a serious girlfriend since he left Virginia. Truth be told, if there was a silver lining to his accident, it was that. He'd missed the companionship of a woman. Longed for someone to share his days—and nights—with. After years of one-night stands, he was hoping to turn over a new leaf. He was nearly twenty-six. The idea of settling down wasn't as scary as it had been when he was twenty-one and thought he was ten-feet tall and bulletproof.

"Jade doesn't have a boyfriend either," Doug suggested.

Daniel had met Doug's cousin. The accident had injured his arm, not his brain. "I think Jade's a bit unbroken for me. She'd be a wild filly to tame."

Doug laughed. "Yeah. Uncle Sawyer says she's ornery as a mule."

Daniel had to agree with that assessment.

"There's always my other cousins, Hope or Sterling. They're not dating anybody either."

Doug's matchmaking was in full-force. "Well, I'll keep that in mind. I haven't had a chance to meet them yet."

"If Sienna wasn't dating Josh, you could go out with her."

Daniel couldn't resist digging for a little info. "You like Josh?"

Doug shrugged. "He's okay, I guess. He doesn't ride horses or rope or anything like that." Daniel could tell by the crinkle in Doug's nose those were big marks against Josh.

"Well, not all guys can be as cool as us."

Doug laughed. "Yeah. You're right. Can I go again?"

Daniel rubbed his shoulder, trying to ease some of the stiffness out. The damn thing was giving him fits today. "Aren't you tired? You've been at this same drill for nearly two hours."

Doug shrugged. "One more time. Please."

Daniel nodded and started the clock. A car pulled down the driveway, distracting him. Sienna was home from work. She was the lone Compton who hadn't fully embraced his arrival here. While she was friendly, he'd had to work hard to engage her in conversation after his playful teasing at his trailer. It had taken days for her to look at him without suspicion or nervousness. Oddly enough, her anxiety pleased him, made him realize he wasn't alone in his attraction.

Sienna Compton was an equal mix of sweet and sexy, with long chestnut hair that was touched with just enough red highlights to match the fiery temper he'd seen the day they'd met. She had dark brown eyes and an hourglass figure that just begged to be admired and touched and caressed and...

Shit. If Seth knew all the inappropriate thoughts Daniel was having about his daughter, his boss would probably kick his ass from here to Mars.

On top of her pretty face and quiet disposition, Sienna was also a puzzle. Daniel had precious few challenges in his life now that his bull riding days were over. There was something about Sienna that called to him, made him long to figure her out.

He'd actually learned more than he cared to about her boyfriend, Josh, from Jade. Jade was a regular around the stable, a born ranch hand. She was tough, opinionated and funny as hell. Daniel had uncovered quite a bit about Sienna through her. Jade's main concern about her cousin was the fact she'd never dated anyone except Josh. In Jade's opinion, See was settling for the first boy she ever loved without bothering to "test drive" different makes and models.

While Daniel couldn't fault Sienna for her loyalty and commitment—he admired both those characteristics—it was her unwillingness to live a little that bothered him. In the two weeks he'd been here, she'd done nothing more than go to work and hang out with her family each night. She constantly followed the same routine of work and home with nothing else to break up the monotony. Jade assured him that pattern wasn't a fluke, but the norm.

Jade complained that her cousin was too set in her ways, and Daniel had to agree. He longed to take Ms. Sienna Compton out of her comfort zone and show her a good time, introduce her to a little spontaneity. From what he could tell, fun was something she was lacking in her life. Hell, it was something that had been lacking in his lately as well.

He lifted his hand in greeting as she emerged from her car. She waved back and then walked over to the paddock when Doug called out to her.

"Hey, See. Watch me!"

Doug returned to the starting line, then asked Daniel to restart the clock.

Sienna patted Daniel's horse before approaching the fence. "Okay, I'm watching."

Daniel gave Doug the nod to begin.

Sienna blew out a long, tired breath. She looked like a balloon with a slow leak, her shoulders sinking.

"Tough day?" he asked, observing her exhausted expression.

"Yeah. There's a flu bug going around. We were booked solid on appointments today. I barely managed to squeeze in a ten-minute lunch break." Sienna worked for one of the local doctors. While Compton Pass wasn't exactly a small town, it certainly wasn't large enough to classify as a city. It boasted five doctors, two dentists, a grocery store and, he'd learned from Sawyer, they'd just added a deputy to the police department, which meant Sienna's uncle was no longer the lone lawman. The nearest Walmart was nearly sixty miles away, something unheard of in Daniel's home state, where it seemed like you couldn't throw a stone without hitting one of the stores.

"Hope you don't come down with the flu."

She glanced up at him. "I had a shot."

He absentmindedly rubbed his shoulder again and studied her outfit, silently amused with himself. He was actually turned on by Sienna's hot pink scrubs. Jesus. He'd gone way too long without a woman. Hell, he hadn't gotten laid since his accident. He'd hit a honky-tonk last night with some of the other ranch hands, but none of the local ladies tempted him like Sienna.

"Does your arm hurt?" Sienna asked.

Daniel stopped moving. "It's a little stiff." He glanced toward the sky. "I suspect we'll have a thunderstorm tonight. One of the benefits of my injury is I can now predict rain with pretty decent accuracy. The weathermen have nothin' on me."

Her gaze locked on his face, studying him in a purely medical way. He wished she'd view him a little less professionally.

"You've been working really hard since you got here. You need to be careful not to overdo it. What were your injuries exactly? You never said."

He shrugged, wondering if there was some way to avoid this conversation. He didn't like to dwell on the accident. It reminded him too much of how much he'd lost. "Dislocated shoulder, right arm broken in three places, four broken ribs, cracked skull and a punctured lung. Those were the biggies. There were a bunch of other smaller issues."

Sienna winced. "The biggies were big enough. I have some salve in the house that will help that sore shoulder. I'll change out of my work clothes and bring it over to your trailer in about an hour. It'll fix you right up. Okay?"

His pride emerged first and Daniel started to refuse, to claim his shoulder was fine and that he had his own muscle cream. Luckily, his brain engaged just in time to save him from refusing her generous offer. "Thanks."

She turned to offer Doug some sound advice on his run before she headed toward the house. Daniel gave Doug a few more pointers and then returned his horse to the stable. He hurried back to his trailer, anxious to tidy the place before Sienna arrived.

They hadn't started off on the best of terms and he was hoping to correct that. He'd just dried and put away the last dish when there was a knock on the door.

He opened it and invited Sienna to enter. "Come on in. I was just straightening up a bit." While he'd thought her nursing scrubs were cute, she was downright hot in her jeans and sweater.

Sienna smiled. "You didn't have to go to the trouble. I'll only be here a minute."

He hoped he'd be able to entice her to hang around longer. She started to hand him the salve, but he didn't reach for it. "Truth is, I have some cream, Sienna. I just don't seem to be able to hit all the sore spots with it."

She eyed him suspiciously. He couldn't blame her. Despite his attempts to play nice, he'd definitely admitted to his interest in her the last time she was in his trailer.

"Daniel, I—"

"You have a boyfriend. I'm perfectly aware of that, Sienna. I'm just asking for a little nursing TLC." It was a lie and a dirty trick. If he'd learned anything about her, it was that she took her job very seriously.

"Fine," she said, gesturing to his upper body. "Take off your shirt."

Daniel couldn't restrain the grin that proved her words had taken his mind straight to the gutter.

Sienna frowned, though he didn't think she was as annoyed as she pretended. Maybe somewhere in the past two weeks she'd begun to soften toward him? "Don't get excited, cowboy. I'm just going to rub some of this ointment on your sore shoulder."

"You know, I'm a firm believer in paying my way. I could return the favor. I've been told I give very good massages and you look like you could use some relaxing after your long day." He took a step toward her, but she stopped him, placing her hand on his chest.

"Your gratitude is more than enough for me." She *definitely* wasn't annoyed. Sienna was smiling, clearly enjoying their flirting dance. Her hand lingered on his chest. Daniel tried to ignore how good it felt there.

"My shoulder is pretty sore. I might need some help with these buttons."

Sienna laughed. "Just take the damn thing off."

He grinned and began to unbutton his flannel shirt. "I think we got off on the wrong foot, Sienna."

Her smile dimmed. "You didn't, but I did. I'm sorry I snapped at you the first day we met. I've been in a really shitty mood lately and you ended up in the line of fire."

He shrugged off his shirt and waited for the inevitable pity. He'd seen it in the eyes of plenty of nurses as he recovered from his injuries. Though the scars weren't quite as red or as angry-looking as they had been right after the accident, they still managed to cut a fairly nasty swath across his pale skin. He hoped when summer arrived, the tan he usually acquired would tone down the paths of destruction wrought by the bull.

Sienna didn't speak for several moments, her face completely inscrutable. Finally, she lifted her gaze to his, her playful eyes capturing his. "Ouch."

Her unexpected joke caught him off-guard, and he laughed. "You can say that again."

She stepped toward him, her close proximity allowing him

to catch a whiff of her floral perfume. Lilacs? Roses? He sucked when it came to distinguishing flower scents, but either way, she smelled damn fine.

"RDL?" she asked, pointing to the small tattoo etched just above his heart.

He glanced down, running his fingers across the letters. "My brother's initials."

"Oh."

"Got the tattoo on what would have been his twenty-first birthday. Might sound corny, but I sort of thought it was a way to show I'd never forget him."

She shook her head. "Nothing corny about that. I think it's a beautiful gesture. My dad and uncles have tattoos on their backs. Amazing ones that represent Compass Ranch. When I was little, I used to run my finger along the pictures on my dad's while he explained what everything signified."

"No ink on you?"

She grinned. "God no."

"Why do you say it like that? Sounds like you like tattoos."

"Oh, I do. I love them. I guess I've just never found anything meaningful enough to have it etched on my skin forever. Suppose I'm still searching for that memory I want to last."

He could understand that. The small tattoo on his chest was his only one. Like her, he believed the sentiment behind the ink needed to be significant. Important.

She pointed down the narrow hallway toward the rear of his trailer. "I assume your bedroom is back there?"

"Won you over with my hot body, didn't I?"

She uncapped the salve and he crinkled his nose at the potent scent. "You wish. This will be easier on the bed."

He wiggled his eyebrows. "Most things are easier on the bed."

She tilted her head. "One more sexual innuendo from you and I'm walking. Got it?"

"Spoilsport."

She laughed as she headed down the hall. "Grab a bath towel if you have one."

He stopped briefly by his small bathroom and plucked one from the rack. Then he joined her in his bedroom. "What's this for?"

"I thought you could lay on it. It'll keep your bedspread from getting sticky." She kept her eyes glued to his face as she spoke, daring him to make another dirty comment.

"You're not playing fair."

Sienna winked. "Never said I would. Lay down, cowboy. On your stomach."

Daniel spread the towel out and crawled to the center of the mattress, while trying to discreetly adjust the hard-on that emerged the moment Sienna had entered his bedroom.

Her knee lightly grazed his hip. He watched as she scooped some of the salve onto her hands and rubbed them together before pressing on his shoulder. Daniel groaned in relief.

"God damn, that feels nice."

She deepened her touch, digging her fingers in and hitting all the right spots. "You're wound up as tight as a spring. Try to relax."

"That would be easier if you'd move those sweet hands a little lo—" He paused, cutting off his dirty joke midstream.

Her hands stopped moving. "A little what?"

"Nope. Not saying it. I don't want you to leave."

She chuckled and began caressing his stiff muscles again. "That bull did a number on you."

He nodded, her soothing massage taking effect quickly. A few more minutes with her talented hands and he'd be sound asleep. "Yeah. I guess so."

"I realize my dad brought you here to help the boys train for their rodeo competitions, but—" She stopped speaking. Daniel waited a few seconds, then he realized she wasn't going to finish.

"But you hate the idea of your brothers growing up to ride the bulls."

"It terrifies me."

He could understand her concerns. "If it makes you feel any better, I don't think James will pursue a life on the circuit. It's just a hobby for him. Sort of like the guys who play football in high school. They're in it for the camaraderie, the fun, not the long run."

Sienna added more balm to her hands, then started rubbing his other shoulder. He didn't bother to tell her that arm was fine. Her caresses were addictive. "It's not James I'm worried about. It's Doug."

"He's young. A million things could come up between now and the time when he's old enough to decide where he wants his life to take him."

His words didn't seem to comfort her. "Maybe. But maybe not. Doug's a lot like me. Once he latches on to something, it's next to impossible to sway him. He seems hell-bent on riding the circuit as soon as he's old enough."

"Does that mean you always knew you'd be a nurse?"

She nodded. "Aunt Lucy swears I came out of the womb with my future predetermined."

Daniel wasn't surprised. "Lucy is the aunt who is a nurse too, right?" Even after two weeks, he was still trying to put names with all the Compton faces. It was a big family.

"Yeah. She is. I used to love to follow her around when she made house calls. She's an amazing caregiver, so compassionate, patient, kind. I spent every summer from the time I was twelve until I graduated from high school as her assistant."

"You're lucky."

"How so?" she asked.

"I never really knew what I wanted to do with my life. Hell, I still don't."

Her hands left his shoulders, moving lower along his back. If he were a cat, he swore to God, he'd start purring. She was working her magic, alleviating every bit of tension in his body, offering him comfort, relieving the pain. Lucy was right. She *was* born to be a nurse.

"You didn't always plan to ride bulls in the rodeo?"

He shook his head once, too lethargic for much more motion than that. "No. I guess I was just your typical kid, full of crazy dreams about futures that wouldn't happen. In elementary school, I told everyone I was going to be a famous football quarterback with a handful of Super Bowl rings. Then, in middle school, I figured I'd make an awesome rock star even though I'd never picked up a guitar and my singing sounds more like frogs croaking."

Sienna laughed. "Wow. There's a perverse side of me that would like to hear you sing."

Daniel grinned. "Seriously toyed with the idea of being a cop in high school, but I have an aversion to guns."

"Really? So you aren't a hunter?"

Daniel knew hunting was a popular form of recreation in Wyoming—for sport and for food—but he'd never felt compelled to go out and kill a defenseless creature. "Nope. Not going to shoot something that doesn't have the ability to shoot me back. Doesn't seem fair."

He glanced over his shoulder in time to catch her impressed expression. "Good for you. Josh and his dad hunt all the time. Before we went off to college, they spent two weeks every fall on these big hunting excursions. The living room in his family's home is filled with deer heads and stuffed turkeys, even a bobcat. It's like *Village of the Damned* in there. Gives me the creeps."

"I can imagine it would." He resisted the urge to point out that if she married Josh it was likely she'd be living in her own creepy animal graveyard.

"So when did you realize you could ride the circuit?" she asked.

He shrugged. "Not sure there was an *aha* moment or if I just sort of fell into it. I graduated from high school and decided to take a year to travel around, see a bit more of this big-ass country of ours. I only made it as far as Colorado. Stopped off to see a rodeo. I'd participated in competitions most of my life, but in the East, it's not quite at the same level as out here. Anyway, I was bitten. Signed up for some amateur shows, won more than I lost. Before I knew it, I was there, riding in the professional circuit. Best two years of my life."

"And then the bull?"

"Yep. Bastard put a period to that career choice."

Her hands stilled, but she left them lying in the middle of his back. They were warm, comforting. "So what now? You plan to be a ranch hand the rest of your life?"

He sat up, facing her. "I haven't exactly figured that out

yet."

She shook her head, a wrinkle forming in the center of her brow. "How can you stand that?"

He chuckled. "Stand what?"

"Just drifting around aimlessly with no direction, no goals."

He tilted his head. "I have a goal, Sienna."

She picked up his towel and wiped her hands on it. "Like what?"

"I want to be happy."

"That's your big goal? To be happy?"

He stretched his shoulders, amazed by how much better he felt, how loose. She'd worked wonders on his tense muscles. "Can you think of a better ambition?"

"I'm not saying that's not a good thing to aspire to, but how do you intend to get there?"

He glanced around his room. "I'm pretty happy right now."

"At Compass Ranch?"

He nodded, though she'd missed his point. "Yeah, I like it here. Like your family and the work."

"Oh."

He shifted closer. "But when I said I'm happy now, I meant this moment, sitting here, with you."

A slight flush painted her cheeks. "Flirting will get you nowhere, Daniel Lennon. I have a boyfriend, remember?"

He nodded, unconcerned by her reminder. Sienna needed a break from her well-ordered life and he intended to see she got it. There was something about the unflappable woman that made him long to ruffle her feathers. "What do you do for fun, Sienna? I've been here two weeks and your life seems to consist of work, home, repeat. Don't you ever go out?"

She shrugged. "I'll go out when Josh gets home. We like to go to the movies or out to dinner together."

He let his sarcastic tone say it all. "Wow."

She scowled. "I'm sure it doesn't sound very exciting to you. I understand you went out with some of the hands last night. Rumors are flying around about you and the blonde waitress at Spurs."

He loved small towns. Never took long to get a reputation. Even one that wasn't earned. "Oh yeah? What are the rumors?"

Her face turned a bright shade of red. "I'm not about to say it aloud, but I'd certainly never be caught dead having sex in a public bathroom. They're filthy."

He couldn't help it. He laughed. He'd been propositioned by the waitress, but he hadn't accepted her offer. Even so, it was more fun to let Sienna think he had. "Are you sure you want to get married, Sienna? Seems to me you may be better suited for life in a convent."

"There's absolutely nothing wrong with keeping my sexual encounters private and with someone that I love."

"Josh was your first, wasn't he?" He knew the answer. There weren't too many subjects Jade considered off-limits and she'd filled in that blank on Daniel's third day on the ranch.

Sienna glanced around the room, unwilling to look him in the eye. "Not that it's any of your business, but yes."

"And you've never been with anyone else?"

She shook her head, still refusing to face him.

"What a waste."

Her gaze flew to his. "It's not a waste. It's beautiful, romantic. We're in love. Who says I have to sleep with a million different men just to have a full life?"

"I'm not suggesting you go out and screw half the men in

Compton Pass. But aren't you curious? Don't you ever wonder what it would be like to take another man to your bed?"

Sienna started to rise, but Daniel caught her hand.

"This conversation is way too personal. You're crossing a line, Daniel."

"No. I haven't even started to cross it yet. But I will." He tightened his grip on her wrist, though the action wasn't necessary. She wasn't trying to get away anymore. "It's like you're frozen in ice, Sienna. You've surrounded yourself with a thick, cold wall hoping it will preserve all the things you think you want and keep you safe from the unknown."

She didn't respond, though he felt the slightest tremor in her hand.

"You're so focused on the end result, you're stifling yourself. Have you ever said to hell with anything? Ever done something crazy without worrying about the consequences?"

"That would be stupid, reckless," she whispered.

"Yeah, it would." He leaned closer, drawing her near enough that he could feel the heat of her breath on his face. "Be reckless," he dared her. "Just once. Right now."

She didn't move, didn't reject him as he closed the distance between them and kissed her. He kept the touch light at first, gentling her as he would a skittish horse. Her lips gradually softened beneath his. He lifted his hand to her face, cupping her smooth cheek with his palm before running his fingers through her long hair.

Sienna's name suited her. There was a fiery red fighting to be released from the muted brown she used to bury her true nature.

She responded slowly but surely. Turning her head slightly, she allowed him to deepen the kiss. Her lips parted and he accepted her silent invitation, his tongue meeting hers halfway. She tasted so damn sweet.

Her hands returned to his bare shoulders, her fingers gripping the muscles in a much sexier massage. It took all the strength in his body not to push her down on the mattress, to cover her body with his and show her the true meaning of recklessness. But he wouldn't—couldn't—do it. She wasn't ready to accept his offer. And if he was a good guy, he wouldn't make it. She had a boyfriend.

He started to break the connection, but Sienna beat him to it. She rose quickly, moving backward until she hit the wall. "Shit. I can't... We shouldn't have—"

He raised his hands in a gesture of surrender. "It's okay, Sienna."

"No. It's not. I don't cheat on my boyfriend. This is wrong."

He couldn't argue with that. He'd been an ass to push her. "I'm sorry. I promise it won't happen again." He prayed to God he could keep that vow. Problem was he still longed to kiss her. Badly.

She studied his face and he suspected she was searching for deceit.

"I mean it, Sienna. I won't touch you again until you ask me to."

"I'll never ask for that." Her voice was shaky.

He was tempted to call her on the lie. She'd ask. He'd make damn sure she did, but until then...

He remained silent.

She looked toward the door, anxious for an escape. "I have to go."

He didn't try to stop her. "Thanks for the salve and the massage."

She nodded, then left without another word.

Sienna rushed from Daniel's trailer, her head whirling. Why had she let that get so far out of hand? She'd never been tempted to let another man touch her, let alone kiss her. So why had she granted Daniel such liberties?

Because you wanted it. You were dying to know what it would feel like to have his lips on yours.

Daniel pushed buttons she didn't realize existed. She'd always thought herself lucky in love. She and Josh were compatible in bed as well as out. It had never been hard for her to achieve an orgasm. Josh was a considerate, patient lover, and she had no complaints.

Until Daniel Lennon showed up at Compton Pass. He made her imagine things she'd never considered, never desired with Josh. She and Josh had learned about sex with each other. They'd both been virgins when they met, so they'd fumbled through, found their own way. Just because they didn't exactly set the sheets on fire didn't mean it wasn't good. It was comfortable, easy with Josh. Sweet.

Daniel struck Sienna as a man who could teach her things she'd only read about in erotic romance books. And suddenly, she was dying of lust, anxious to try them.

It bugged her that while she'd never longed to try those things with Josh, the same didn't hold true for Daniel. Her body physically ached every time they were in the same vicinity. Her nipples tightened, her pussy tingled and her skin flushed.

Josh would be home in a few weeks. God. If she could keep her libido under control until then, she could get some of this pent-up sexual frustration out of her system. Maybe she'd even suggest to Josh that they spice up their vanilla sex life. Then she'd convince him to come home for Christmas so they could really explore some new things. She could do this.

She had to.

"Where are you going in such a hurry?"

Sienna jumped, startled when Jade emerged from the stable. "Jesus!"

Jade threw her hands up. "Sorry. Didn't mean to scare you."

Sienna put her hand over her heart, trying to calm it. It had been racing since she left Daniel's trailer. "It's okay. I didn't see you there."

Jade glanced to the left, following the direction Sienna had come. "Where were you?"

Sienna considered lying, but it was pointless. Jade could read her face too well. "Daniel overdid it today working with the horses and then teaching Doug barrel racing techniques. I offered some salve to soothe his stiff shoulder."

Jade smiled. "Only the salve or did you rub it on too?"

Sienna rolled her eyes. "I'm a nurse, Jade. He was in pain and I helped alleviate it."

"I bet there are a few other pains in Daniel Lennon's body he'd let you ease if you'd let him."

"Don't be vulgar."

"A little dirty fun with Daniel might be just what you need. I bet that man could teach you some new tricks. And it's obvious he's into you."

Sienna frowned, disagreeing with Jade's assessment. "Daniel's into women in general. He's a player. I'm sure you've heard the rumor about Lacey going down on him in the bathroom at Spurs last night. Hell, you work there. You must've seen it."

Jade rolled her eyes. "It's a complete lie. Lacey caught sight of Daniel when he came in with the hands. She likes to mark her territory whenever a hot new buck comes to town. She followed him to the bathroom all right, but I'd bet Compass Ranch nothing happened. For one thing, there wasn't enough time. Secondly, I saw Daniel and Lacey's faces when they came out. She was putting on a good front, but I could tell she'd been rejected, and he was annoyed, plain and simple."

Sienna wondered why Daniel didn't attempt to clear his name when she mentioned the rumor. "Regardless of what he did or didn't do with Lacey, I'm not interested."

Jade grinned. "Really? Tell me again, Sienna. When did you go completely blind? That guy is sex in blue jeans. I wouldn't mind taking a tumble with him in the hayloft. I hope to hell he's still here during the summertime. What's he look like without his shirt on? Bet he's built like a brick shit house."

"You need to stop hanging out with ranch hands all the time."

Jade didn't back down. "Don't hold out, See. Put me out of my misery."

Sienna recalled the scars on Daniel's chest. They seemed to make him uncomfortable. "He's okay."

Jade laughed. "You're such a shitty liar."

"This whole conversation is pointless. In case you've forgotten, I'm in a relationship. I'm not about to throw away what Josh and I have for a roll in the hay with some cowboy who probably won't be here come spring."

"Remind me again. What is it you and Josh have exactly?"

"What's that supposed to mean? You know damn well we're committed to each other. Our futures are set. Together."

Jade smirked. "I understand that you think so, but I'm starting to doubt whether or not Josh is still on board with the

Sienna Life Plan. Have you asked him lately?"

Sienna tried to ignore the little voice in the back of her head that said Jade was right. Josh had been distant since returning to college this year without her. She blamed it on the miles and the fact they were both busy, but her gut instinct told her it was more than that. "It's not my life plan, Jade. It's ours. Josh is as committed to me as I am to him."

Jade stuffed her hands in her front pockets and started walking toward her car. "I hope that's true. I gotta go. I'm bartending at Spurs again tonight. See you tomorrow."

Sienna watched her cousin climb into her car and drive away. She reached up and touched her lips, recalling Daniel's kiss. There was a part of her that couldn't deny it was the best kiss she'd ever had.

God. When did life get so complicated?

And exciting?

Chapter Three

Daniel helped Jody and Vicky clear the supper table. Since the invitation to join them for dinner his first night on the ranch almost a month earlier, he'd found himself offered a regular spot.

"Thank you," Jody said when he put a stack of dirty plates in the sink and began rinsing them. "I know you're here to help the boys improve their rodeo skills, but do you think you could add kitchen duties to that list? I wouldn't mind Doug and James learning how to pitch in around here."

Daniel grinned. "I'm afraid I was pretty hopeless at all this stuff until I moved out of my parents' house and started doing it for myself. My mom tried to assign it to me as a chore, but eventually she gave up when she realized it would only be done right if she did it herself. I never did learn how to load a dishwasher to please that woman. No matter how many times I tried."

Vicky chuckled. "The washing machine gene seems to be lacking in the Compton males as well. Last time Doug tried to help me, he had all the dinner plates facing the wrong way."

"I think you mean dishwasher, Vicky," Jody corrected.

"What did I say?"

"Washing machine," Daniel replied easily.

"Oh," Vicky chuckled. "Well, the men in this family struggle with that appliance too."

They all laughed.

Sienna entered the kitchen and tossed a dishrag in the sink. "Table's wiped up. Need any more help in here?"

Jody shook her head as she put the last few pieces of silverware in the sink. "No. I think Vicky and I have everything in hand."

"We sure do appreciate all your help, Levi," Vicky said as she grabbed the coffeepot, filling it with water."

"Levi?" Sienna asked. "Vivi, this is Daniel."

Vicky was silent for a moment. "Oh, my goodness. I'm sorry, Daniel."

Jody laughed. "Man, that's a blast from the past. Levi hasn't worked here in nearly a decade. Wonder what made you think of him, Vicky."

"Who knows?" Vicky shrugged nonchalantly, but Daniel could see she was disturbed by the mix-up. She'd called him by the same wrong name a couple days earlier, but he hadn't bothered to correct her. He could only assume Vicky had seen a lot of hands come and go during her fifty years on Compass Ranch.

Jody put detergent in the dishwasher. "Daniel, if you've got a few minutes to hang out with See and the guys, I've made a coconut cream pie for dessert."

Daniel rubbed his stomach. "Few more weeks here and I'll need to buy bigger pants. Even so, it's a sacrifice I'm willing to make for a piece of your pie."

He followed Sienna into the family room. Seth and the boys had plopped down on the large sectional and were watching a hockey game.

"Who's playing?" Daniel asked as he took a seat.

"Kings and Rangers."

Sienna claimed a comfortable chair near him, curling her legs beneath her. Since kissing her in his trailer two weeks ago, Daniel had made sure to keep his distance—physically—but that didn't mean he hadn't worked to regain her trust while building a friendship.

They all sat in silence for a few minutes until the Kings scored. Doug and James were rooting for L.A., so they started trash talking with Seth, a Rangers fan. Sienna smiled at their antics but didn't take part.

"You like hockey?" Daniel asked her.

She shrugged. "It's okay. I prefer it over baseball or basketball. Unfortunately, these guys—" she gestured to her brothers and dad, "—watch it all. I don't think I've ever actually held the remote control in this house. Not once."

"You ever think about getting your own place? You're working now. I'm sure there must be an apartment near the doctor's office you could afford to rent. That way you'd have control of the TV."

She dismissed his suggestion. "I'm fine staying here and saving my money until Josh graduates in the spring. We'll probably rent a place for a few years, but with me working and living at home for now, we'll have a down payment for our own home sooner than we'd planned. I guess that's one benefit to him changing his major and staying in school an extra year."

"Yeah, but isn't that extra year going to add to his student loans?" Daniel wondered about Sienna's boyfriend, uncertain why he disliked the guy so much. Over the past two weeks, he and Sienna had spoken every night, always in the company of her family. Each time the subject of Josh had arisen, Daniel had learned something else about the man that annoyed him.

Sienna shook her head. "He won't have any debt at all. His parents are paying for his education."

Daniel fought to keep his face impassive, though her answer bugged the hell out of him. Another tick against Josh. He was spoiled.

Seth must have been listening to the conversation because he said what Daniel was thinking. "If I were his folks, I'd have made him start footing the bill this year. I think Josh would benefit from having to work for what he wants."

Sienna didn't reply. Daniel got the feeling this conversation wasn't a new one.

Seth gestured to Sienna. "Take my baby girl there. She kept a 3.9 grade point average in college and held down a part-time job to help pay her way through school. She didn't take her education for granted because she knew how much it cost and how hard she had to work to earn that money."

"Dad," Sienna said, "Josh appreciates his parents' help. It's not like he's wasting their money. He's getting an education that will help them manage the store better."

Seth shrugged, letting the argument lie, though Daniel noticed his boss didn't agree.

Daniel was curious to meet Josh, to see the guy who'd earned Sienna's unwavering loyalty. She sure did spend a hell of a lot of time defending her boyfriend's actions.

He let his gaze drift over her. She was wearing the same royal blue sweater she'd worn to his trailer when he'd kissed her. It made her chestnut hair seem redder, brighter, more vivid. He'd always been a sucker for a redhead and while he wouldn't call Sienna's hair auburn, she had just enough of the color to catch his attention. The sweater hugged her curves, showing off her generous breasts.

He shifted in his seat and willed away the erection

threatening to make an appearance. What an idiot. He was sitting five feet from his boss and getting a boner from staring at Seth's daughter. Daniel had worked hard to keep his attraction to Sienna a secret, but tonight he feared he was failing in the attempt.

Stupid.

First of all, he needed this job. Pissing Seth off didn't seem particularly smart. Secondly, Sienna was committed to a jerk boyfriend who obviously didn't deserve her. While he longed to shake up her well-ordered life, to show her there was a world full of men who would treat her better, Daniel couldn't do that as long as she was with Josh.

Sienna's phone beeped. Glancing at the screen, she stood. "Speak of the devil." Daniel caught sight of Josh's smiling face as she clicked on the screen. "Hi, Josh," she said, her voice lighter and breezier than Daniel had ever heard it.

Then Daniel heard Josh's reply and was forced to acknowledge he sounded like a nice guy.

Hey, beautiful. Damn, you're a sight for sore eyes.

"Sweet talker," Sienna teased as she left the room.

Seth's attention returned to the game. Daniel tried to concentrate on the TV, but he found himself straining to hear Sienna's voice. She'd only walked to the hallway. While he could hear her tone, he couldn't make out the words she was saying. Everything seemed fine for a few minutes and then he heard her say something louder, with definite anger.

"What do you mean it's too late?" she asked.

Her voice drowned out the TV. Seth glanced toward the hallway. He sighed heavily, allowing Daniel to see that he wasn't exactly pleased with his daughter's boyfriend.

"Sounds like the asshole screwed up again," Seth muttered.

"Is this a pattern?" Daniel asked.

"It is lately. I'm not sure what's gotten into the kid. Josh always had his head screwed on straight, and he was good to Sienna. Then, last year, out of the blue, something snapped. He decided to change majors and his grades started slipping. More often than not, they end up fighting whenever he calls. He's coming home next week for Thanksgiving. I'm going to have a word with him. This shit's not going to fly for much longer. I don't like him upsetting Sienna all the time."

Daniel was glad to hear Seth had plans to talk to Josh. He'd been wondering lately if there was a way he could warn the man off, but considering Daniel had only known Sienna a month, it really wasn't his place.

Given the dark expression on Seth's face, Daniel was grateful he wasn't going to be the recipient of that little talk. Seth, a peaceful, fair man, had a protective streak a mile wide when it came to his kids.

Daniel noticed it went quiet in the hallway. Then he heard the front door open and close. Worried about Sienna, he stood. "I think I'll take a rain check on that pie. I'm still full from supper." It was cold as blue blazes outside. Clearly, Sienna was upset if she'd decided to brave the elements rather than return to the warmth of the family room. He needed to make sure she was okay.

Seth's gaze drifted from Daniel to the doorway. Daniel tried to ignore the way his boss's eyes narrowed slightly. "It's pretty dark out there. Be careful."

The last two words, though innocent enough, seemed to hold a deeper warning. Shit. He was falling for the boss's daughter.

The first time he'd laid eyes on her, Daniel had felt too strong a pull to the pretty, though far too serious woman. In the past, he'd chosen women who preferred a fun time over commitment, a few quick tumbles in the hayloft versus a long, drawn-out wooing.

Sienna was the complete opposite of his type. She was a nice girl, but it didn't matter. He ached to drag her to the dark side with him, to draw out some of the wickedness he sensed lurking beneath the surface. And maybe, just maybe in the midst of all that hot sex, she'd find a way to bring some sort of order to his own fucked-up life.

"I'll be fine, Seth. Good night," he said.

James and Doug waved goodbye absentmindedly, their gazes never leaving the television. Seth, however, watched him depart, suspicion written on his face. Something told him he was going to wind up getting one of Seth's little talks after all.

As he stepped onto the front porch, he paused to let his eyes adjust to the darkness. He scanned the yard, seeking Sienna, and caught sight of her heading down a narrow path that led to the creek.

He pulled his coat around him and cursed the cold. Then he followed her direction, his speed and long legs cutting the distance between them quickly. When he got within earshot, he called out her name.

"Sienna."

She stopped walking and turned, waiting until he caught up.

"What are you doing out here?" she asked.

He tried to play it casual. "I was heading back to my trailer. Isn't it a little cold for a stroll in the moonlight?"

She shrugged. "I needed to cool off."

"Trouble with Josh?"

"He's failing business calc."

Daniel paused, pleased that she'd answered his question. In the past few weeks, he'd felt a friendship building between them. Unfortunately, he wasn't going to be happy just being her pal. "Isn't the end of the semester coming up?"

"Yeah. It is. He has less than a month to bring up a very low grade. If he doesn't manage that, then he'll have to stay at college this summer to make up the course."

He could understand her frustration. Sienna had been ready to start her new life as an adult when she graduated last spring. Now she was putting her future on hold while Josh played catch-up. "Can't he get a tutor or something?"

She nodded. "He could. If he would. I made that suggestion a month ago, when things were still salvageable, and he didn't bother. Now he seems to think it's too late."

"Does Josh *want* to graduate from college?"

Sienna laughed. Her expression instantly morphed from pissed off to unadulterated humor. The sound had an unexpected effect on him as his cock began to thicken. He needed to get laid or else he'd do something very stupid, like make a play for the boss's unavailable daughter. "I'm starting to think he doesn't. Josh seems very resistant to entering the real world."

"And that's funny?" He couldn't understand why she was laughing about the situation.

"Nope. It's annoying, frustrating, maddening. But if I don't laugh, I'll cry, and there's no way I'm going to shed any more tears over Josh's stupidity."

He knew it. Her fucking boyfriend had been making her cry. Daniel's hand balled into a fist. His decision was made. Seth wasn't the only man on the ranch who'd be having a little talk with Josh next week.

He took a deep breath and tried to calm down. "Seth said

he's coming home for Thanksgiving."

"He is. And he and I are going to have a come to Jesus meeting."

Daniel hoped she was going to direct her immature boyfriend to the nearest exit, but he didn't think she would. "Meaning?"

"It's time for Josh to grow up. His parents aren't going to keep footing the bill for him if he fails course after course."

"It's not just his parents who are being inconvenienced. What about you?"

She glanced up at the moon, then she sighed. "I'm in this for the long haul. He probably sounds like an idiot to you, but that's because you've never met him. Josh is actually very sweet. I really think he's just going through a phase right now. We'll have a long talk over Thanksgiving and everything will be fine."

Daniel didn't think so, but he wasn't sure how to argue with her. He *didn't* know Josh. Regardless, he was damn sure the guy didn't deserve Sienna.

Her face cleared. "Thanks for talking things out with me, Daniel. I feel better now." She rubbed her gloved hands together for heat. "I think I might head back to the house for some coffee and pie. Are you sure you don't want some?"

He shook his head. "No. It's getting late. I'm going to turn in early."

"Good night," she said.

"Night, See." He watched her walk back to the main house, but he made no effort to return to his trailer. She'd been right about one thing. The cool air helped him think too.

As for the rest...

Well, she'd been wrong about all of it. Regardless of how

sweet Josh was, he was wrong for Sienna Compton. The asshole was stifling her, holding her back from her true potential.

Daniel smiled. It was time for a new plan.

Chapter Four

"That was a damn fine meal." Daniel rubbed his too-full stomach as he walked into the Comptons' family room, surprised to find Sienna alone. Josh had arrived earlier this morning. Daniel thought he'd sensed some tension between Josh and Sienna, but he chalked it up to wishful thinking on his part. Much as it pained him to admit, Josh seemed like a nice guy.

Loud conversations from the dining room carried to them. The house was jam-packed with Sienna's family celebrating the Thanksgiving holiday. He'd gotten to know all of her aunts, uncles and cousins over the past month, but now his head was reeling as he tried to remember the names of all the close family friends who were visiting.

"The Mothers can cook." Sienna stressed the word *mothers*.

"Mothers?"

Sienna laughed. "It's a nickname Jade gave to my mom, Leah, Lucy and Cindi. When they come together, it's like they morph into this huge giant force that takes out everything in its path. There's pretty much nothing that goes on in the family that isn't discussed at length by all of them every Sunday afternoon at *teatime*." Sienna used air quotes around teatime.

Daniel was confused by her gesture. "What's wrong with *teatime*?"

"I've never seen one of them drink a cup of tea. They usually make a pitcher of margaritas or split a bottle of wine."

He chuckled. "Your family is hilarious. Never seen a family who gets along like this one, never fighting, always having fun."

"You say that now, but you better hope you never fall into the Mothers' sights. There's no subject they don't consider themselves authorities on, and once they've discussed your so-called problem at length, they'll offer endless advice. They've rearranged the furniture in every house on this ranch, helped plan more parties than I can count and set up way too many blind dates."

"Wow. And I assume this drives everyone crazy."

Sienna shook her head. "Nope. That's the most annoying part of it. They have amazing decorating taste, create menus to die for and, while I won't say their matchmaking record is perfect, it's pretty damn close. Don't get me wrong, I love my mom and aunts to death. It's just that sometimes it's hard to accept their advice, even if you think it may be right."

Sienna didn't have to explain. Daniel assumed her strained relationship with Josh hadn't just caught Seth's attention. The Mothers would have noticed as well.

"What did they tell you to do about Josh?"

Her eyes narrowed. "How did you know that's what I was talking about?"

He grinned. "Not that hard to figure out."

She sighed. "It's been suggested that I have a conversation with Josh about his intentions for the future while he's home this weekend. They think it's time we nailed down some particulars. And Aunt Leah is also concerned about my all work, no play lifestyle. I'm sure I have Jade to thank for getting Leah riled up about that."

"So are you going to talk to him?"

Sienna didn't have a chance to respond before Vicky entered the room. "There you are, Sienna. Have you seen my red tablecloth? I'd planned to put it out on the dessert table."

Sienna frowned. "Vivi, you asked me about that a few minutes ago. I told you we don't have it anymore. It was ruined last Christmas when Doug spilled grape juice on it. We threw it out, remember?"

Vicky nodded. "Oh, that's right. All this cooking has me worn out. It must have slipped my mind." Though she played it off, Daniel saw the confusion on the older woman's face as she left the room.

Sienna ran her hand through her hair anxiously. "Damn. She didn't remember that first conversation at all."

"No. I don't think she did."

"She's forgetting a lot of things lately."

Daniel shrugged. "Probably just a sign of age. Didn't you tell me she was turning seventy this year?"

Sienna glanced at the doorway where her grandmother had just left, her face pensive. "Yeah, she is. But she's been forgetting too much lately."

"Alzheimer's?"

She frowned. "God, I hope not. While there have been some advances made in terms of diagnosing and treating different types of dementia, there's still a long way to go. If it's that..." Her voice drifted away as if she was frightened by the possibility. "I'm going to talk her into getting a checkup. There are some tests I'd like the doctor to run on her."

"That's not a bad idea," he said softly before her attention was captured by something else in the hallway. Daniel caught sight of Josh putting on his coat before going outside.

He glanced at Sienna's face. She didn't appear too anxious to follow her boyfriend. "Looks like the time might be right for your conversation."

"Yeah. And here I thought the chances of me getting him alone today were slim to none." Sienna made no move to leave.

Daniel reached out. Sienna's brow crinkled, but she took his proffered hand. He grasped her cool fingers and gave them a reassuring squeeze. She was visibly nervous. "Things are never as bad as you fear."

She didn't try to release his hand. "Were you afraid when you got on that last bull?"

He nodded. "I was afraid every time."

"Then why do it?"

He winked at her. "Why not?"

She laughed lightly. "God, there is something seriously twisted inside you."

"Turns you on, doesn't it?" He pulled her closer, leaning down until his face was level with hers. He couldn't resist teasing her, trying to replace some of the anxiety he saw in her eyes with humor. "I told you, See, if you want me to kiss you again, all you have to do is ask."

She dropped his hand and shoved him away, laughing. "You're ridiculous. And conceited. And insane. I'm going to go talk to my *boyfriend*."

"Go get 'em, tiger."

She paused at the door, but didn't turn around before continuing out. It didn't matter. He heard her chuckling in the hallway.

"Where's Sienna going?" Doug asked.

"She and Josh are headed to the stables to see the new horses your dad's bought."

Doug tilted his head. "Josh hates horses. Is that code for having sex?"

"No, it's not code. Besides, what do you know about sex?"

"I'm eleven years old, Daniel. I'm not a kid."

Daniel nodded in acknowledgement. Doug was constantly fighting to prove he was a man. "There's nothing wrong with being a kid, Doug. Life's a hell of a lot easier when you are."

Doug wasn't buying it. He shrugged, his face becoming far too serious for someone so young. "Maybe. Do you wanna have sex with Sienna?"

Daniel choked. "What? Why would you ask me something like that?"

"You two look at each other all the time."

Jesus, all this time, Daniel had been worried about letting Seth see too much. Turns out he should have been shielding his interest in Sienna from her baby brother. Then, something Doug said clicked. "She's looking at me?"

Doug rolled his eyes, taking on the long-suffering tone of someone trying to explain something that's obvious to an idiot. "Only all the time. When she sets the table for supper, she puts your place next to hers, instead of mine, like I tell her to. And she comes to the stable to talk to you after work. She never did that before. James said it's 'cause she's got the hots for you. I'm not stupid. Hots means she wants to have sex with you, which is pretty gross, by the way."

"Thanks for the definition." If Daniel wasn't so floored by Doug's revelations, he'd fist-bump with the kid. Then he realized Doug didn't look very thrilled by the prospect. "Would it bother you if I was interested in Sienna?"

Doug didn't answer immediately. Instead he tilted his head, lifted one shoulder. "I dunno."

Doug, for all his rough and tumble ways, was very protective of his older sister. Suddenly the boy's disdain for Josh made sense. Doug didn't like the idea of his sister with any man.

Before Daniel could figure out how to set Doug's mind at ease, they were interrupted.

"Hey, Doug," Austin, one of Doug's cousins, yelled from the hallway. "We're going outside to shoot targets with my new BB gun. You comin'?"

Doug's eyes brightened, and it was clear the sex talk was over. "See you later, Daniel."

The young boy sprinted toward his cousins without a backward glance, leaving Daniel alone again. He drifted toward the front window and glanced at the stable. For weeks, he'd gone against character and left Sienna alone to sort out her life instead of pursuing what they both obviously desired. Hell, he hadn't even given the upper hand to her. He'd given it to Josh, the tool.

Time was up on this bullshit. Daniel was about to toss his own hat into the ring.

Sienna walked out to the stable, searching for Josh. He'd been quiet most of the day. While it was hard to get a word in edgewise whenever all the Comptons got together, Josh usually made at least a bit of an effort.

She suspected he was feeling the same strain she was. After all, Josh—despite growing up in ranch country—was not fond enough of horses to brave the cold just for fun. Time to bite the bullet.

"Josh?"

It was quiet for a moment before she heard him say, "Over

here, See."

She followed the sound of his voice and found him sitting on a bale of hay, his back against the stable wall. He looked tired.

"What's up?" she asked.

He patted the hay bale next to his. She sank down, her heart aching as she realized just how badly the next few minutes were going to suck. She'd been so wrapped up in all the things she wanted to say to him, practicing her speech for days, that it never occurred to her that Josh might be as unhappy as she had been lately.

"Listen, Josh—"

"No. Wait, Sienna. I have something I need to say and I'd just like to get it out, so let me go first, okay?"

She nodded.

"I haven't been the best boyfriend lately."

She started to brush off his words, even though they were true. Josh waved her denial away. "Don't. Don't pretend like I haven't hurt you. I have."

"I wish I knew what was going on inside your head, Josh. We always used to be on the same page. I never had to work so hard to figure you out."

He chuckled, the sound holding no mirth. "I wish the same thing. I feel like I'm floundering around these days, constantly trying to find a way to make you and my parents happy while deciding what to do. Unfortunately, I'm failing at everything—school, life, you."

"It's okay. You just need—"

"I need a break."

Sienna paused. "A break? From what? School?"

He shook his head. Realization dawned hard.

"Me?" she asked.

"Sienna. I've loved you since I was fifteen years old. We grew up together, always as a couple. I have no idea what it means to be my own man."

She'd known what was coming the moment she entered the stable. So why was it so hard now that he was saying the words she'd anticipated? The words she'd even planned to say herself? The stubborn part of her—the part with no sense—reared up. "I don't understand. I've been with you for seven years too. I know who I am."

"Do you?"

Such a simple question. Two words. And yet they set Sienna's world on end.

Did she?

Daniel would say no. Hell, he'd only been on the ranch a week the first time he'd called her out for her fears. Seen right through her.

"So you're breaking up with me?"

Josh shook his head. "No. God no. I don't want to lose you. I just think we need a break. A few months to find out who we are without each other."

She frowned. "That doesn't make any sense."

"I plan to spend my whole life with you. I swear that hasn't changed for me. We're going to be happy, I'm sure of that. But I'll always wonder what else there was. What if there's an experience I miss because I never had a chance to look around?"

Sienna's sadness gave way to annoyance. She'd put her life on hold for Josh. Made excuses for him, defended him to her family and friends when they said he was being irresponsible. She felt like she was stuck in a game of Freeze. Josh had yelled the word and she'd stopped in place, not moving a muscle while he ran around and did whatever he pleased. It rubbed against the grain. "Spell it out for me, Josh. What exactly are you asking for?"

"To be free. To take a break from having a girlfriend for a little while."

He was being purposely obtuse. It was so like him. To speak in generalizations and hope she wouldn't call him on it. After so many years together, he should have known better. "So you plan on sleeping with other women."

Josh winced, but he didn't deny it. "Haven't you ever wondered what it would be like with someone else?"

A couple of months ago, her answer would have been an unequivocal no. Then she remembered Daniel's kiss. The way he cupped her face as he pressed his lips to hers. That simple touch had rocked her to her core and she'd spent too many nights since then waking up in a cold sweat, her body aching for more.

Suddenly, she felt very tired. In the past, she would have fought with Josh, refused his request, pushed him for all or nothing. It was probably what she should do, but she didn't have the energy. She wasn't sure she felt like struggling for this relationship anymore. And that thought hurt more than Josh's desire for a break.

His request was preposterous, the idea that he was actually sitting next to her asking for permission to screw around completely obnoxious. And yet, she was going to let him get away with it.

She was going to give him this timeout because she needed one too. He wasn't the only one with a bit of soul searching to do. "Fine."

"What?" Josh's shocked expression almost made her laugh.

"We'll take a break." She didn't put any parameters on it because she couldn't think of any. Josh's silence proved he was waiting for her to plot it all out, discuss the details, point out the fine print, but no words came.

"That's it?"

She nodded.

"But what about—"

"Josh. We don't need to think this to death. Let's just go with the flow."

Josh blinked several times. She assumed he was studying her face to make sure it was really her. She resisted the urge to reassure him she hadn't been abducted by aliens. When she didn't add anything more, Josh stood. His stiff posture proved he was still waiting for her to pull the rug out from under him.

"I decided to go to Florida with my roommates for Christmas."

She nodded, rising to stand next to him. "Sounds like fun."

He frowned. "Are you sure you're okay with this?"

She reached out and grasped his hand. "I'm fine. Honest. I should probably get back inside or my family will send out a search party when I don't show up for Vivi's pumpkin pie."

Josh squeezed her hand. Then he used it to drag her forward for a kiss. The kiss, though gentle and sweet, didn't move her. It didn't make her heart race. It didn't do anything. It was passionless, platonic, boring. Then she realized Josh's kisses had felt like this for a long time.

"I'm coming back for you," he whispered. "I swear it."

She nodded, but she couldn't find it in her heart to promise to be waiting when he did. She honestly wasn't sure she would be. Her eyes were wide open and seeing too much. Everything.

"I should head home and spend some time with my parents

since I won't be back for the holidays."

"Okay. Goodbye, Josh."

"I'll see you over spring break, Sienna."

He turned and left, but Sienna remained in the stable. For the first time in her life, she didn't have a clue what she was supposed to do next.

Daniel stepped into an empty stall as Josh passed. If he'd been any sort of gentleman, he would have walked away as soon as he realized Sienna and Josh were still talking. Unfortunately, he couldn't make himself leave. He didn't trust Josh not to hurt her and if he did, Daniel intended to be close by, ready to catch her if she fell.

Only she hadn't fallen.

He stepped out of the shadows and walked to where Sienna stood, motionless. Her gaze lifted when she caught sight of his face. He must have given away too much because she rolled her eyes.

"Eavesdropping, cowboy?"

She clearly wasn't angry, but her voice didn't carry the usual teasing tone he liked so much. It just sounded empty.

"I didn't mean to."

She snorted. "It's not hard to avoid. You just turn around and walk away."

He didn't bother to deny how much he'd heard. "Are you okay?"

She nodded. "Josh wants a break."

"Yeah. I heard. That doesn't bother you?"

She bit her lower lip, a line forming in the center of her brow. "I don't think it does. Maybe it will tomorrow, when I've had time to process it all. Right now, I'm kind of in shock. At some point, I'll have to figure out what it means, what I'm supposed to do now."

Daniel took a step closer. "Or you could do what you suggested to Josh. Go with the flow."

She gave him a sad grin. "I have a feeling I'll hate that."

"Depends."

"On what?" she asked.

"On who you're flowing with. Josh asked for his freedom and you gave it to him. There's something you need to remember about that. You're free too."

She crossed her arms. Daniel assumed the gesture was more for protection than warmth as the stable blocked out most of the chilly November air. "I guess so. Only problem is I didn't necessary want to be free."

Sienna walked back to the hay bale and kicked it—hard—stirring up dust. "God, I'm such an idiot. The man I plan to marry just asked for permission to screw around. And I gave it to him. I must seem like the world's biggest fool to you."

Daniel didn't like seeing her so hurt. Walking behind her, he wrapped his arms around her waist in a gentle embrace. "Turn around, Sienna. Look at me."

She twisted in his arms slowly as her face lifted.

"The only jackass in this barn was Josh. He'll figure that out one day, but it's going to be too late."

"Why do you say that?"

Daniel placed a soft kiss on her forehead. "Because by the time he's finished sowing his wild oats and ready to come home, you won't be here waiting for him."

She frowned. "I have no intention of leaving Compton Pass. Josh or no Josh. This is my home."

Daniel ran his finger along her cheek. "That's not what I meant."

She started to question him, but Daniel wasn't willing to waste the time explaining. Better to show her.

His first kiss was brief, but powerful. Sienna needed to understand there was a world of difference between him and the man who'd just left.

Their lips parted for only a second.

Long enough for her to whisper, "Oh."

Then he kissed her again, refusing to hold back any of the desire he'd spent weeks stifling. Sienna Compton needed to go wild.

And he intended to be the man who really set her free.

Chapter Five

Sienna glanced out her window, studying the moonless night sky. A week had passed since Thanksgiving, and she'd taken the coward's way out. She'd holed up in her bedroom every night after work rather than risk seeing Daniel, too afraid of succumbing to the temptation he provided.

She'd given seven years of her life to Josh. Wrapped her world around him, and it wasn't easy to let go of that. Despite how much Josh's need for a break hurt, there were still too many good years—memories—to mourn. When she added the recollection of Daniel's amazing kisses to her mixed-up thoughts, it felt like she was on system overload.

Her family was worried about her sudden retreat, though they'd allowed her the space. Mom brought her dinner on a tray each night, offering a soft kiss on the brow and her assurance that things would get better. Doug usually kept her company for an hour or so before his bedtime, filling her in on his school day and his rodeo lessons with Daniel. Even her dad had stopped by two nights ago to check on her and to tell her he loved her. His sweet words had been her undoing and she'd curled into his arms and cried out all her pain against her daddy's strong chest.

Despite the love and support of her family, Sienna still struggled to pull herself out of her funk.

"Knock knock."

Sienna spotted her grandmother at the door. "Hey, Vivi."

"Thought I'd check to make sure you still live here. The house isn't nearly as nice since you went into hiding." Vivi planted herself on the bed, patting the mattress to encourage Sienna to sit next to her.

"I'm not hiding." It was a lie, but Sienna felt compelled to tell it anyway.

"Of course you are. But that's all right. I suspect you needed a wee respite from real life. You ready to come back yet?"

Sienna felt like she should protest, but unfortunately there was too much truth in her grandmother's observation. She sank down next to her grandmother. "I don't have a clue what I'm supposed to do next."

Vivi nodded. "I'm sure you don't. And I'm glad."

"Glad? Why?"

"Because for the first time in your life, you're facing an uncertain future. That's not a bad thing, Sienna. In fact, it's perfectly normal. I think of all my granddaughters, I've always worried about you the most."

"You must be kidding. What about Jade's recklessness or Hope's shyness? God, Vivi, Sterling is so damn impulsive, you never know what she's going to do next."

"And yet, they'll all be fine because they've learned to roll with the punches. They've taken risks in their lives and they've survived the fallout. You're twenty-two, Sienna, and you've never suffered a broken heart until this moment. You've never faced any true adversity or trouble. You set your course at a very young age and you marched toward it without a single misstep."

Sienna grimaced. "You don't think Josh was a misstep?"

"Do you?"

Did she? Even though she was hurt and pissed as hell, she worried about the small part of her she knew would take him back if he called tomorrow to say he'd changed his mind. She hated that part. It made her feel cowardly, weak, shallow.

"So what do I do now?"

Vivi took her hand and squeezed it. "That's yours to figure out."

Sienna closed her eyes. "That's your advice. Figure it out?"

Vivi pressed her forehead to Sienna's. "You expected something wiser?"

"Uh, yeah. Jeez, Vivi, you're nearly seventy. Surely you've learned something in all that time that could help me."

"Maybe I have. Did I ever tell you about the night I met your Granddaddy JD?"

Sienna shook her head. "No. I don't think so."

"We met at a barn dance over in Clarke. That's where I'm originally from. JD was in town visiting a neighbor of mine for a few days. I swear the second he walked into the barn, every woman's head turned to stare at him. JD was handsome as the devil, with jet-black hair and eyes as dark as midnight in the mountains."

Sienna had seen pictures of her grandfather. Vivi's description was accurate. "He was totally dime."

Vivi laughed. "You girls and your funny words for things. I can remember when Jody used to say Seth was a hottie. I assume dime means he was good-looking?"

Sienna nodded, her grin growing wider. "Yeah. But don't ask me why."

"It wasn't just JD's appearance that caught my eye. It was

the way he held himself."

"I guess so. He was huge." Sienna could recall her mom referring to JD as a gentle giant.

"That's not exactly what I mean. Sure, you would expect such a tall, broad-shouldered man to make an impact when he entered a room, but it was even more than his size. It was his personality, Sienna. JD was a commanding presence."

"He sounds really cool. And a little bit scary."

"That's a perfect description of how I felt when I saw him. I was attending the dance with my beau, Charles."

"I didn't realize you had a boyfriend when you met Granddaddy."

Vivi nodded. "Oh yes. Charles and I had dated for well over a year, and I doubt there was anyone in Clarke who wasn't expecting wedding bells in our future. Charles had dropped hints about us getting married and, at the time, I'd been pretty sure that was what I wanted too."

"Granddaddy JD changed your mind?"

Vivi seemed to relive the memory as she told Sienna the story. "He did indeed. JD's gaze took in the barn, studying every person there, but he stopped when he saw me. It's a cliché, but the moment his eyes captured mine, it was as if time stood still."

Sienna sighed. "Sounds romantic."

"It was. He walked straight over to me, never taking the time to notice that Charles was standing right beside me. He said, 'My name is JD Compton. Would you care to dance?'"

"And you said yes."

"Of course I didn't. I informed him I was Vicky Murphy and that I was attending the party with my boyfriend, Charles. Then I suggested that he find someone else to dance with."

Sienna's eyes widened. "What did Granddaddy say to that?"

"He bowed slightly and apologized. While his words were nothing but courteous, I knew I was still in trouble."

"Why?"

"Because JD gave me this infuriating, meaningful smile that let me know he had not been deterred."

"And obviously he wasn't. So what happened then?" Sienna asked.

"Charles and I danced together a few times, but my gaze kept drifting to JD. It didn't seem to matter where he was in the room, my eyes followed. He asked a couple different girls to dance and I tried to ignore the jealousy that ran through me when he smiled at them, making polite conversation. After a little while, Charles went outside for a smoke. The band played a faster song and a conga line formed. I hopped in, grabbing the waist of my cousin, Shirley. A few seconds later, a pair of hands touched me. It was like I'd been struck by lightning. I didn't have to turn around to realize whose hands they were."

"JD's."

Vivi nodded. "The train grew longer with people laughing as they moved around the room. Unfortunately, Shirley took one turn a bit too sharply and I lost my footing. JD's grip tightened, preventing me from falling. I stepped away from the train and JD joined me, his arm still wrapped around my waist. He leaned close and said, 'I've got you, Vicky Murphy. I won't let you fall.'"

Sienna pulled her pillow to her chest. "That's so sweet."

"And such a lie," Vivi said with a grin.

"What? Why?"

"Because I did fall. Right at that moment. And JD did nothing to prevent it. Just let me tumble head over heels in love with him."

"What about Charles?"

Vivi's attention turned back to Sienna, her eyes suddenly serious and sad. "I was a bit stubborn in those days and set in my ways."

"In those days?" Sienna teased.

Vivi playfully tugged Sienna's hair. "Very funny, Miss Pot. Meet Miss Kettle. You do realize you get your stubbornness from me."

"Mom says I get it from my dad."

"And where do you think Seth got it?"

They laughed together.

"Can I continue with my story?" Vivi asked.

Sienna gestured for her to go ahead.

"Regardless of what my heart knew to be true about JD Compton, my head wasn't going down without a fight. It's funny how we can trick ourselves into thinking we're perfectly content, simply because it's easier than taking a chance on finding true, genuine happiness."

Sienna suddenly understood the point of Vivi's story. "You think I was settling with Josh?"

Vivi shook her head. "I can't answer that question. Only you can see what's in your heart."

"What if Josh is the one who'll make me happy? What if I let him go and I never find anyone who makes me feel the way he did? I mean, he hasn't always been an idiot."

Vivi didn't laugh at her joke. "No. He hasn't. And I'm not sure he's being one now. He's been quite honest with you when you think about it. He's confused about where he's going. Rather than lie or cheat on you, he came to you and asked for time. That couldn't have been an easy thing for him because he does care about you. And let's face it, my dear, you tend to hold the upper hand in that relationship."

"I do not."

Vivi rolled her eyes. "Sienna Compton. You have too much of your mother's blood running through your veins to ever play the meek woman. For seven years, you've made the decisions and Josh, God bless his patient heart, has been willing to follow your lead."

"Daniel kissed me. Twice." Sienna wasn't sure why the words fell out at that particular moment, but she felt like she needed to come clean to someone.

"I see. And?"

"And I liked it. A lot."

"But?" Vivi prodded.

"But I'm scared. I've never been with anyone except Josh. We're comfortable and life is so easy when we're together. I don't know anything about Daniel Lennon."

"You know you like the way he kisses."

Sienna frowned. "He has no plans for the future. He's drifting from day to day with only one goal. To be happy."

"Sounds like something we should all aim for."

"But what about his family? And who knows where he intends to settle down. *If* he intends to settle. I mean, for God's sake, his house has wheels. That doesn't seem like someone who'd be content to live in Podunk Compton Pass forever. And regardless of how screwed up the rest of my life may be, I'd never be happy anywhere but here."

Vivi shook her head. "Don't you think you're jumping the gun?"

"What do you mean?"

"You've leapt from a man kissing you to planning out the

rest of your lives together and worrying about whether or not it'll work."

Sienna sighed. "Crap. You're right. Why do I always do that?"

"Apparently you're asking for advice, so here it is. There's nothing wrong with having goals and plans, but life is much more fun when you take chances as well. Try to live in the moment for a little while, Sienna. Take each day as it comes without worrying about tomorrow. Can you do that?"

Could she? Sienna honestly wasn't sure, but she was willing to give it a try. "Okay. I guess so."

"Good," Vivi rose, walking to the doorway. "Oh, and Sienna, no more hiding. Life is happening out there, not in here."

Vivi left, and Sienna realized her grandmother hadn't finished her story. What happened to Charles? How did Granddaddy JD finally convince her to take a chance with him?

Sienna started to follow her grandmother to ask, but pulled up short when she caught sight of herself in the mirror. Her hair was tied together in a messy ponytail and her eyes were puffy from too many nights of crying.

Time to get yourself together, Sienna.

What do you want?

Only one thing popped into her mind.

Daniel.

Sienna opened her dresser drawer, rummaging through the panties and bras until she found what she sought. Tugging the tags off a new, sexy nightie, she held it up in front of her. She'd bought it for herself last Christmas, but she'd never worn it. Never found an occasion special enough to share it with Josh. God, had she really been unhappy for so long?

Sienna removed the rubber band, letting her hair fall loose

around her shoulders. Bending forward, she ran her hands over her face as a new plan fell into place. In theory, it was simple.

In reality...

Jesus. She tried to summon her nerve when she considered what she planned to do. When that failed, she called the queen of impulsiveness, Sterling.

Sterling's face appeared on her phone. It was only when she noticed Sterling was in her sleep shirt, sitting on her bed, that Sienna realized how late it was.

"What's up, See?"

"Sorry. Did I wake you?"

Sterling shook her head. She still lived with Uncle Sam and Aunt Cindi in their little cottage through the woods. The path between Sienna and Sterling's homes, as well as the one that led to Hope's house, was well-worn. One of the nicest things about living at Compass Ranch was how close she was to her cousins. They were her best friends, and she couldn't image how different her life would have been without them in it.

"I need help."

Sterling sighed softly. "Are you still upset about Josh? Because if so, you should call Hope to talk about it. She's more forgiving than me. Right now, I'd like to punch him in the face for being such a shithead."

Sienna grinned. Sterling and Jade always had her back. It was a nice feeling. "I don't want to talk about Josh. It's Daniel."

Sterling's eyes widened, interest dawning. "What about him?"

"I'm planning to sleep with him, but I don't know how to initiate it. I mean, short of walking to his RV and stripping off all my clothes."

Sterling's mouth fell open. Sienna wasn't sure she'd ever

seen anyone actually gape until that moment. Part of her was pleased she'd been able to shock her unshakable cousin.

Then Sterling went into motion. "Conference call."

Sienna shook her head, but it was too late. She could see Sterling plugging in Jade and Hope's phone numbers.

Dammit. She'd hoped she and Sterling could keep this conversation between them. Then she heard her mother's voice in her mind. Jody often mourned for the good old days when phone calls were just between two people and you couldn't see who you were talking to. Her mother was always one of the last holdouts whenever it came to technology.

In the meantime, Sienna and her cousins had begged their parents to buy them the latest and greatest each and every time a new phone came on the market. Usually Sienna loved the ability to talk to—and see—all of her cousins at once. This was especially true during the years Sienna was away at college. She'd missed her cousins so much those four years. Being able to see their faces and hear their voices over the video phone never failed to chase away her homesickness.

Unfortunately, this wasn't one of those times. Hope's face appeared first. Like Sterling, she was dressed for bed, sitting propped up against pillows. No doubt she'd been reading some juicy romance novel on her ereader. "Everything okay?"

Sterling nodded. "Yeah. We're just waiting for Jade to pick—"

Jade's face appeared. The four of them each graced a corner of the flat phone screen. Unlike Sterling and Hope, Jade was clearly out and about rather than in bed.

"What's wrong?" Jade asked. Sienna heard someone in the background ask for another beer. Jade turned away from the screen for a moment and told the guy he'd had enough and she was cutting him off for the night. Then she yelled over her shoulder, "Bruce. I'm taking a smoke break."

Jade didn't appear to wait for permission. Instead, the background changed as they watched her leave the crowded bar and head for the back door.

"You don't smoke," Hope pointed out.

"So what? It didn't take me too long working here to figure out the waitresses and Bruce were getting more breaks than me just because they're all chain smokers. Fuck that shit. Told Bruce it wasn't fair and that I'd be taking smoke breaks too."

Sienna laughed. "What did he say to that?"

"What could he say? I'm right and he knows it."

And if Bruce didn't realize it at first, Sienna had no doubt Jade drove the point home relentlessly until the man gave in simply to shut her up.

Jade had clearly made it to the parking lot as Sienna spotted several cars in the background. "Listen, as much as I'd love to have one of our virtual slumber parties, I'm going to have to go back in soon. So cut to the chase. What's wrong?"

Growing up, Jade had felt like odd girl out because she didn't live on the ranch. In order to keep her in the group, they'd started holding weekly virtual slumber parties—sometimes with their parents' knowledge, sometimes without. They'd crawl into their own beds, then fire up the conference call, giggling and whispering until the wee hours.

"Sienna's going to sleep with Daniel."

Sienna winced at Sterling's abrupt announcement. "Actually, I was only thinking about it. I'm not sure that I'm going—"

Jade rolled her eyes. "Dear God. Please stop thinking. I swear I'll hang up right now if you tell me this is just another Sienna *should I, shouldn't I* gab-fest."

Once again, Sterling answered for her. "It's not. She's going to do it."

Hope smiled. "I think that's awesome. Daniel is gorgeous and funny and smart and so nice to your brothers."

Hope's list went a long way to easing her fears, but deep inside, Sienna still wasn't sure she had the nerve to go through with it.

"Great, Hope," Jade interrupted. "But FYI, none of that matters. This is just sex, right, Sienna?"

Sienna nodded quickly. That was the only part of this whole crazy scheme she was certain of. She'd just gotten out of a long-term relationship, if Sienna could call her "break" from Josh getting out. In reality, she wasn't sure she was out at all. She and Josh had dodged the conversation at Thanksgiving, settling nothing.

The only thing she knew for sure was she wanted to have sex with Daniel. Her heart wasn't ready to jump into anything else, but her body, well, that was a different story. Daniel had uncovered her previously undiscovered libido and, since she was a free woman, she didn't see any harm in exploring the uncharted territory. "It's just sex."

"Well, then the answer is simple. Shower, shave, makeup, lingerie." Jade consulted the time on the phone. "It's almost eleven now. You can be at his RV by midnight."

"Tonight? Oh no. I wasn't even considering—"

"It has to be tonight, Sienna." Sterling's assurance took her aback.

"Why?"

Hope smiled sympathetically. "Because we know you. If you don't go now, you'll lay awake all night making a list of reasons why you shouldn't. And then tomorrow..."

Hope shrugged, letting Sienna fill in the unspoken *you won't go*.

She started to argue, promise them she'd follow through with the plan later, but they were right. The words died on her lips.

Vivi's advice drifted through her mind.

Live in the moment.

Sterling piped in with her own advice. "And don't get nervous and start babbling."

"I don't do that," Sienna protested.

Hope giggled. "Remember your college graduation party when Uncle Seth suggested that you say something to everyone?"

Sienna tilted her head haughtily. "I hate public speaking."

Jade laughed as well. "It was just family and a few close friends from town. I'd hardly call that public."

"There were nearly sixty people there and they were all looking at me," Sienna clarified.

"And you rambled for close to twenty minutes, thanking basically every single person you'd ever met in your life as well as the guy who delivered the booze." Sterling shook her head. "When you get anxious, inane words fly out in a steady stream."

"Fine, I'll keep my mouth shut."

"Um, Jade," Sterling said suddenly.

Jade was standing with her back to the parking lot. Hope's eyes went wide as Sienna grinned. "Yeah?"

"Don't turn around," Sterling instructed.

If there was one thing they all knew about Jade, it was that they should never tell her *not* to do something. To do so was the equivalent of a dare and Sterling knew it.

Jade glanced over her shoulder just in time to spot crazy Stanley's bare ass as he mooned her.

"What the fuck are you doing?" Jade yelled as Sienna, Hope and Sterling burst into loud laughter.

Stanley turned around before he hitched his pants back up, treating them all to more than an eyeful of his shriveled penis. "Serves you right for not getting me another drink, Jade Compton."

Jade appeared to forget she was on the phone as her face disappeared from her portion of the screen. The rest of them were treated to fleeting glimpses of cars, the bar, bits of Jade and Stanley as she shook the phone at him. Sienna felt faintly motion sick watching it.

"You get your hairy ass and tiny dick out of here before I call my dad and have him arrest you for indecent exposure, you fucking pervert!" Jade yelled.

Stanley must have taken her threat to heart as Jade's face reappeared on the screen.

"Thanks a lot, Sterling. Now I'll have to scratch my eyes out to try to get that image out of my mind."

Sterling showed no remorse, her smiling face far too delighted. "Hey, I saw it too."

"Bitch. I have to get back inside. Go over to Daniel's tonight, Sienna. Get laid. Then call me tomorrow with the details." Jade's screen went black before any of them could say goodbye.

Hope tried to stifle a yawn. "I need to go too. Good luck, Sienna."

"Thanks." Sienna glanced at Sterling.

"So. Shower, shave, makeup, lingerie and shut up. Anything else?"

Sterling smiled. "Just let go, Sienna, and enjoy the moment. That's really all there is to it."

Chapter Six

Daniel lay on his back, staring at the ceiling. He refused to look at his clock again. At last check—no more than five minutes earlier—it had been midnight. He'd ticked off every hour since he'd crawled into bed at nine and he was still no closer to finding sleep.

Eventually, sheer exhaustion was going to have to win out. God knew he couldn't keep going at this rate. It had been a week since he'd kissed Sienna in the stable. He would have tried to steal more than a few heated kisses from her, but Sienna pulled away when they'd heard someone enter the stable.

Daniel shuddered to think how close Seth had come to catching them. Even though they were standing a proper distance away from each other when Seth approached, he still sensed his boss was suspicious. For one thing, Sienna's face had been flushed, her gaze roaming everywhere to avoid her father's questioning stare. She may as well have stamped the word *guilty* on her forehead.

Since then, Seth had kept a very close eye on where he was and who he was with. Not that Seth had needed to be on his guard. Sienna was doing a good enough job staying away from him without her father's interference. He hadn't caught more than a glimpse of her when she came home from work each day. She'd stopped eating dinner with the family and even eschewed riding her beloved mare, Maria.

According to Doug, Sienna was depressed over Josh. Daniel knew that reaction was natural, but it didn't stop him from wishing she'd open her eyes and see him as a suitable replacement.

"Fuck that," he muttered. He didn't intend to replace Josh. He wanted to erase him from Sienna's thoughts forever. He wasn't sure when his intentions had changed, but somewhere along the way, he'd stopped hoping to just get into Sienna's pants. Lately, he'd been thinking it might be nice to find a way into her life, but that didn't seem possible.

For one thing, she'd just gotten out of a relationship. There was no way she was ready to hop right back into one. And secondly, he'd heard her conversation with Josh. They hadn't broken up—not officially. They'd just taken a timeout. Daniel didn't think Sienna would let the idiot come back, but, well, dammit, he wasn't sure.

He released an annoyed breath and forced his eyes shut. He'd never fall asleep at this rate. He tried to clear his mind of Sienna Compton completely.

A knock sounded on his door.

"What the hell?"

He listened again, wondering if he'd imagined it or if it was the cold winter wind knocking a branch against the trailer.

Another knock. Someone was definitely outside.

He rose and slipped on a pair of sweatpants. Opening the door slowly, he was surprised to find Sienna, wrapped in a coat and shivering.

"Sienna? Get in here. It's freezing out there."

She quickly climbed the three stairs, passing him as he

closed the door.

"Is something wrong?" He couldn't imagine there was anything—short of bad news—that would bring her to his trailer at this time of night.

She shook her head. "N-no. Everything's fine."

"Okay. That's good."

She didn't bother to explain more. Instead, she shrugged off her coat. Underneath she was dressed in a little slip of a nightgown. He hadn't realized until that moment that her legs were bare. She'd walked all the way over here in a bit of silk and slippers. Obviously she was paying for the decision, given her uncontrollable shivering.

"Jesus, Sienna. What the hell are you wearing? Or *not* wearing? You'll be lucky if you don't get frostbite."

She rubbed her hands together, blowing on them for heat. "This was a lot s-sexier when my cousins and I p-planned it from the warmth of my bedroom."

"Sexy?" Her words hit him like a sledgehammer to the forehead. "Did you come over here to sleep with me?"

Her cheeks were red from the cold, but even so, her blush enhanced the color. "If you h-have to ask, then it's s-safe to say I'm not doing s-so well."

He laughed. He couldn't help it. She was here because she wanted to have sex with him? He'd never been offered such a delectable frozen treat. Unfortunately, she mistook his response.

She reached for her coat, intent on putting it back on. "This was a mistake."

"Oh, hell no. No mistake." He pulled the coat away from her and tossed it onto his couch. Then he tugged her into his embrace, trying to infuse her trembling form with some of his own body heat. He rubbed her back lightly.

"You're warm," she murmured against his chest.

"And your hands are like ice cubes."

"Sorry." She tried to step away, but he stopped her, gripping her wrists. He placed her palms on his chest, holding them there.

"Don't pull away. Let me warm you up."

They stared at each other for a few hushed moments, as Daniel allowed his gaze to travel over her silky nightie.

"Say something," she whispered.

He shook his head. "No. You first. Ask me, Sienna. Ask me to touch you, to take you. I promised I wouldn't do that until—"

"Touch me," she interrupted.

Daniel didn't wait for her to say more. He reached for the hem of her sexy nightie and drew it over her head. Sienna gasped.

"Wait," she said, her hands flying to cover her bare breasts.

"No more waiting. I've wanted you for too damn long. Hell, since my first day on Compass Ranch. Ever since you stood in the trailer and called me out for being a bad son."

She wrinkled her nose. "I said I was sorry about that."

He grinned, his hands gripping her waist for fear she'd come to her senses and try to leave. After weeks of dreaming about this, he was hard-pressed to keep from touching her.

"This is just sex."

He scowled at her clarification. For one brief, foolish moment, he considered refuting her condition. Luckily, his mama didn't raise a fool. "Fine."

"Just this one time."

He shook his head. "No. We can keep it casual, but we're

not putting a time limit on it."

She bit her lip, and he wondered if that would be a sticking point for her. Finally, after too many nervous heartbeats, she said, "Okay."

"I'm only going to ask once, Sienna, and then you'll never hear these words from me again. Are you sure?"

She didn't reply for several painfully long seconds as she studied his face. Then, she nodded slowly.

He turned her toward the hallway that would lead them to his bedroom. With a gentle hand on her back, he propelled her forward. "This will be easier on the bed."

She offered him a sexy grin. "Most things are," she teased, throwing back the exact same words they'd said to each other the day she massaged his shoulder.

He kissed her gently when they entered the bedroom, his hands stroking up and down her bare arms. Her skin was soft, almost silky. When they broke apart, she glanced at the bed, nervously. He longed to take away her anxieties, to make her forget everything except this moment. "Come on," he said. "Let's lay down."

Sienna crawled onto the mattress, then rolled onto her back. He didn't move to join her, as two things collided in his mind. She may have come here to have sex with him, but she was shy as a virgin on her wedding night.

Another strike against Josh. In seven years, he'd failed to bring out Sienna's passion, her fire. Any fool could see it was bubbling beneath the surface, searching for an outlet.

He joined her on the bed, quick to resume their kissing. He lied to himself when he said he was taking things slowly to ease her into this. The truth was, he wanted this night to last. He was in no hurry to see it end.

They kissed for several long, heated moments as Daniel softly stroked her body, touching her face, caressing her neck, rubbing her back.

Sienna's breath was hot against his cheek when he embraced her, giving her a tight hug. "Ready for more?"

She nodded, though he sensed the slightest bit of hesitance.

Daniel tugged at her tiny panties, but the task was made difficult by the fact Sienna's legs were pressed together. He ran his hands along her thighs until she relaxed.

Once the panties cleared her ankles, he tossed the little scrap of cotton to the floor. His hands drifted to her hips. "Open your legs, See."

Her breathing accelerated, but she did as he asked. Her bare body was everything he'd imagined and more. Her hips were round, her breasts full, with rosy, tight nipples that begged to be sucked.

He lowered his head and planted a soft kiss on one nipple and then the other. Sienna's back arched, silently asking for more. He opened his lips and gave her breast a more thorough kiss.

As he sucked on her nipple, he reached down and ran his hand along her slit. Shit. She was dry as a bone. His fingers stilled.

"I'm sorry," she said.

Daniel lifted his head. "Why?"

"I'm not sure why I'm so nervous. I swear to you I want to be here, with you, doing this. Please don't stop. I need this so much. More than I can say. It's just..." She paused. "Shit. I'm rambling."

Her inexperience touched him. He felt humbled by the trust

she was offering. "There's no rush, Sienna. We've got all night. What do you say we take some time getting used to each other?"

"How?"

Daniel grinned. "Just follow my lead." He bent his head and kissed her once more. He'd missed her lips this past week. Though he'd only had a few tastes of her, he intended to make up for it now. Sienna's lips softened, then parted. He dipped his tongue inside, swallowing her quiet moan of pleasure. He was determined to ease her anxiety.

One of her hands moved along his chest, her trembling fingers tightening against his waist as she twisted and shifted closer to him. Sienna pressed her breasts against his torso, clinging to him.

Daniel ran his fingers through her hair. She smelled like strawberries, the scent fresh and clean. He didn't rush, didn't bother to move them to the next level. He loved kissing her, exploring her mouth, trying to provoke her innocent little sounds.

He moved a breath away. "You're so beautiful."

She smiled, granting him another quick kiss before pressing her cheek against his. "Your face is rough."

"I can shave if it's hurting you."

She shook her head. "No. I like it."

He kissed her smooth cheek, reveling in the differences between them. Her softness fit perfectly against his hard body. He continued moving, running his lips and tongue around the rim of her ear before traveling to her neck.

Sienna shivered with desire when he nipped her shoulder blade. "God, this is so incredible," she whispered.

He took her words as an invitation to continue, pushing her

to her back once more and drifting lower until his lips found her breast. Cupping the flesh, he took her nipple between his lips and sucked gently, until his own overpowering needs took over and he increased the pressure. Sienna's head flew back against his pillow, but she didn't try to escape his sensual hold.

He released her nipple with a pop, then moved to offer the same torment to her other breast. Unable to resist, he nipped at her hard nub.

"Ow," she gasped.

He lifted his head to study her face. "Sienna?"

"I can't figure out if that feels good or if it hurts."

He grinned at her confession, then bent his head to bite her other nipple. Her fingers flew to his hair, gripping it tightly. "Holy shit. I decided. It's good. Do it again." She directed his head back toward her breasts and he granted her request for more.

Over and over, he sucked, licked and nipped until Sienna was thrashing beneath him, begging for more.

"Daniel," she said at last, using her hands in his hair to pull his face to hers.

"Not yet." He gave her a quick kiss, then moved down her body. Her legs parted easily this time, and he didn't bother to hide his grin. "Lost your shyness, I see."

He didn't give her a chance to reply. Instead, he lowered his head to her pussy, dragging his tongue along her now wet slit.

Sienna's hips jerked. Daniel placed his hands at the juncture of her thighs, holding her open as he dove in for another taste. He used his tongue, intent on dragging every drop of pleasure from her. He pressed against her clit, tickling the sensitive nub as she gasped for air. Dipping inside, he was met by even more of her sweet juices.

Sienna cried out loudly. "Ohmigod. So fucking good. Josh never... That... I..."

Daniel moved quickly, raising himself until he covered her body, his face inches from hers. "He's not here, Sienna. He's never going to be here. Not with us."

She blinked rapidly, surprised by his hair-trigger response to her mindless chatter. "I'm sorry."

He shook his head. "I don't need your apology. I want you with me. Just me."

"I am. I swear."

He studied her face. "I get that this is new for you, but I'm not planning to help you bide time until Josh comes to his senses. If we start this affair, it's about you and me. And no one else."

She licked her lips. "Okay. Take off your pants."

He grinned. "Nope. Not until you come."

She frowned, clearly confused. Daniel released a disgusted sigh. He'd asked her not to make comparisons, but he was struggling not to curse her ex-boyfriend's lack of skills himself.

He resumed his place between her legs, dipping his tongue into her—once, twice, a dozen times more. Sienna pushed her hips up, trying to drive him deeper, faster. He could taste her need...and her frustration. Lifting her legs, he bid her to hold them higher. She gripped her knees, tugging them closer to her shoulders.

The new position opened her to him. Opened everything. He teased her clit for a moment longer, then he moved lower. Much lower.

Sienna's grip slipped when he ran his tongue around the rim of her anus. He glanced up, trying to read her face. Her shocked—but not appalled—gaze met his. He licked her again.

She trembled, arousal racking her body.

Reaching for her, he brought his fingers into play, pushing two inside her drenched pussy.

"Yes," she hissed.

Daniel moved his fingers in and out several times, trying to ignore how fucking tight her pussy would feel against his cock. He'd promised her an orgasm before he took her and he intended to make good on that. But damn if he wasn't paying for it. His dick was throbbing.

With his other hand, he began to rub her clit. Despite the restraints he saw her struggling to keep in place, Sienna's body began to move, to demand more.

He wondered if she'd ever allowed her passion free rein. Let go of all her inhibitions and just gone wild. It was time someone gave her a push in the right direction.

Removing his fingers despite her complaints, Daniel dragged them lower. He pressed one wet digit against her anus. She shivered, but didn't resist.

Slowly, he used the moisture from her pussy to ease his way. Sienna's thrashing on the bed calmed as her attention focused on his actions.

"Does it hurt?" he asked.

She nodded. "A little, but it's that nice hurt again."

He smiled. Jesus. She liked her pleasure laced with pain. He was only touching the tip of the iceberg here. His mind raced over all the sexual places he intended to take her.

Daniel bent forward, nipping her clit. Sienna gasped, jerked, then groaned as his finger sank deeper into her ass. Time was up. His cock was about to burst. Driving his tongue inside her pussy while thrusting his finger in her ass, Daniel fucked her until she cried out. Her orgasm slammed into her fast and hard, her pussy clenching.

Sienna's hands slipped from her legs to the bed. She fisted the sheets, seeking purchase as one last powerful shudder rattled through her.

Daniel knelt, watching as she melted into the mattress. She was boneless, thoroughly replete. It looked good on her.

He stood, reaching for the waistband of his sweats. Sienna's eyes drifted open when he left the bed. Her gaze lowered as he pushed his pants over his hips. She captured her lower lip in her teeth, and he thought he saw a glimpse of nervousness reappear.

"Sienna?"

Her eyes flew up, met his. "I promised I wouldn't make comparisons, but, um, that's..." She seemed to search for the words. "You're a lot... Fuck." She pointed at his cock. "I think that might hurt."

He chuckled, then crawled onto the bed. "Oh, hey, cock comparisons where I come out on top are always fine."

She laughed. "God. I can't believe I'm here."

He gave her a quick kiss on the brow. "I'm glad you are."

"I am too. So glad." She placed her palm on his cheek, studying his face.

Daniel's cock brushed her hip. His patience was in tatters. Reaching behind him, he rummaged in his nightstand for a condom. He was surprised when Sienna took it from him. Opening the package, she rolled the rubber along his cock so slowly, he saw stars behind his eyes. She was teasing him, but it felt too fucking amazing to stop her.

When he was fully sheathed, he rose above her, his weight resting on his elbows. Sienna opened her legs, wrapping her ankles around his waist. Daniel reached down and placed the head of his cock at her opening.

Neither of them spoke as he pressed inside. If he'd been in less agony, he would have entered her with more care, slowly. As it was, he wanted her too much and she felt wonderful.

Sienna didn't complain, didn't give him any reason to doubt she was with him in her need. Her nails dug into his back as he pushed in the last inch, seated to the hilt.

Then he lifted his hips until only the head of his cock remained and thrust in harder. Sienna's gasps, her moans of pleasure, her fingers clinging to his arms urged him on. Over and over, he pounded inside her as she joined him in the dance. Every time he returned, she was there, her hips lifted to welcome him back. When he felt his climax building, his balls tightening, he reached down to rub her clit.

"Come with me."

"I already came."

Daniel didn't have the strength to roll his eyes, though he sure as hell wanted to. "Do it anyway."

He stroked her clit faster, increasing the power behind his thrusts into her body. Sienna's back arched.

"Holy shit," she breathed. "Holy, holy shit."

Unable to hold off any longer, Daniel's cock exploded, the pleasure so pure, so intense, it couldn't be described as anything less than sweet agony. He'd only begun to come down when he felt Sienna tumble over the cliff again.

Her inner muscles tightened around his cock and he groaned, his flesh too sensitive.

"Fuck." He gasped for air, his chest rising and falling like a horse that had just been put through his paces.

Sienna shuddered when he pulled out and fell to her side. She lay on her back, staring at the ceiling as she attempted to catch her own breath. Daniel watched the veil of uncertainty and shyness begin to cover her again.

He wasn't having it. Rising, he went to the bathroom to quickly dispose of the condom and then he crawled back into bed.

"Come here." He reached for her, wrapping her in his embrace. They were both sweaty, sticky. He was going to insist she take a shower with him.

He knew Sienna would try to retreat to her own bedroom soon, but he wasn't about to let her walk out in the cold winter air in her present overheated state.

She wrapped her arm loosely around his waist, though her body was definitely tense.

"Relax." He reached down to raise her arm higher on his chest, then he lifted her leg over his hips. He liked the feeling of her snuggled against him.

"What are you doing?" she asked.

"We just had some pretty incredible sex. Don't you think we deserve a little bit of cuddling?"

"I have no idea what the proper protocol is after casual sex."

"It's this," he assured her.

She didn't loosen up. Instead, she lifted her head to glance at the clock beside his bed. "I should probably get dressed and head back to my house."

He grinned at her innocence. She was a breath of fresh air after far too many jaded buckle bunnies. He lifted his alarm clock up and set it. He showed her the time. "That early enough?"

She nodded. "You don't mind me sleeping here?"

He tightened his arm around her and kissed the top of her

head. "Close your eyes, Sienna. I'll make sure you're home before anyone realizes you were gone."

"Okay. It *was* incredible, wasn't it?" Her sleepy question told him she was in no condition to fight him about returning home. He was glad. For the first time in a week, he was damn tired himself and there was no way he'd let her walk back to her house alone in the middle of the night.

"That was just the beginning. We're not finished by a long shot."

He felt her lips lift into a grin against his chest. "I'm glad. I have a whole list of stuff I was hoping to try."

"Oh yeah? Like what?"

The tension in her body began to fade as she whispered her fantasies to him. Whether it was the dark room, the haze of sex still lingering in the air or pure exhaustion, Sienna held nothing back as she shared her deepest, darkest desires with him.

His sweet nurse had an active, vivid, sexy-as-hell imagination. Despite having just come, Daniel felt his cock twitch when she described her favorite capture fantasy. He closed his eyes and let her words wrap their way around his own needs, feeding them. Sienna dreamed of bondage, sex in public, being chased, spanked. Jesus.

When her words came slower, he realized she was talking herself to sleep. He gently placed his finger against her lips.

"Shh. Go to sleep, beauty." She was going to need her rest. Because Daniel was determined to give her everything. He'd fulfill all her fantasies.

And then he'd give her more.

Chapter Seven

Sienna sat on the front porch, rocking slowly on the swing. While her eyes were taking in all the happenings of the ranch, she wasn't seeing a damn thing. It was her day off. She'd intended to use the time to do a little Christmas shopping, but she couldn't manage to wrap her head around the holiday.

After a week of sneaking out for midnight rendezvous with Daniel, she was tired, sore in places that had never hurt before and flying so high off the ground, she couldn't see Earth.

So far, she and Daniel had managed to keep their change of status from friends to lovers a secret from her immediate family. Only her cousins knew. She smiled when she recalled the very long group grilling she'd received after her first night in Daniel's RV.

She'd never seen Jade so impressed and, if she wasn't mistaken, Sterling had appeared a bit jealous. *Of her.* It was fun to be the wild Compass girl for once. For the first time in her life, she could see the appeal of cutting loose, having fun, living on instinct.

She and Daniel had agreed to keep their relationship a secret because neither of them was sure how her father would react. Daniel needed his job and, given the fact Sienna had never dated any boy besides Josh, there were some unknowns in terms of how far she could push Dad's protective streak. Sex with a boyfriend was one thing, but a casual affair with one of his ranch hands? Sienna had no desire to approach her father and say, "Oh, by the way, Dad, I'm sleeping with Daniel. But don't worry. It's nothing serious. Just fucking."

Vivi and Hope walked out onto the front porch.

"There you are," Vivi said, joining her on the swing. Hope claimed a rocking chair nearby. Vivi and Hope had a standing weekly lunch date. Usually, Hope would pick her up and take Vivi out somewhere special, but as their grandmother had just started to recover from a head cold, they'd opted to stay in today.

Sienna grasped her grandmother's hand. "Did you two have a nice lunch date?"

Vivi nodded. "We sure did. Hope's chicken salad is officially better than mine. My reign as ruler of the kitchen is over."

They laughed, then Vivi lifted her face and took a deep breath. "The fresh air feels good. It's a pretty day."

Sienna agreed. They were having a brief respite from the chilly weather. Today's sunshine actually felt warm for a change. "That's one reason why I decided to hang out here rather than tackle the shops. Unfortunately, I'm afraid I'm going to pay for that later. I still don't have Christmas gifts for James or Dad."

Vivi pulled her sweater around her, her legs moving in time with Sienna's as they rocked on the swing. "Your mom and I went in together to buy your dad that new saddle he's had his eye on. That man will buy the boys the best of everything when it comes to riding equipment, but he never manages to get himself anything nice. I swear he's used the same saddle for nearly twenty years. I can't believe the thing hasn't fallen apart."

Sienna nodded. "Yeah, that's true. Maybe you and mom are

on to something there. I'll talk to Daniel to see if there's anything else Dad's using in the stable that could stand to be replaced."

Hope spent a few minutes listing all the things she'd bought for her family. Sienna grinned as she listened. Hope was the queen of Christmas. She usually had her shopping finished and her presents wrapped before Halloween. While Sienna wasn't quite that efficient, she was typically in better shape by this time of the year. If she didn't get her act together soon, she'd be doing the Christmas Eve dash with Jade and Sterling. Something she never thought she'd have to do.

It had been a weird winter. Hell, the whole year had been screwed up. And yet, Sienna couldn't muster any regret or sadness. Truth be told, she was having the time of her life.

Vivi smiled. "Sounds like you found some really nice things, Hope. Jody and I got Seth a new saddle. I can't wait to see his face when he opens the box. That one he's using now is about to fall apart."

Hope gave Sienna a funny look before turning her gaze back to their grandmother. "You just told us that, Vivi."

"Oh. Did I?" Vivi frowned as warning bells sounded in Sienna's head.

Sienna leaned closer. "I'd like to make you an appointment to come in and see Dr. Spencer."

"Why?" Vivi asked. "I just had a checkup six months ago."

Sienna nodded. "Even so, I'm concerned about these lapses of memory you keep having."

Hope chimed in. "I think a checkup is a great idea."

Vivi waved away their concerns, dismissing their anxiety with a joke. "You're worrying for nothing. When you get to be my age, you're lucky if you can remember your own name most days."

"Even so, I'd feel better if you'd go," Sienna pressed.

Hope bent forward, resting her elbows on her knees. "So would I."

"No," Vivi snapped, rising from the swing angrily. "There's not a thing wrong with me and I don't appreciate you girls pestering me. My memory is fine."

Hope bit her lip nervously. Sienna shared her cousin's surprise and anxiety. Vivi had never lost her temper with them. Ever.

"Vivi," Sienna started, trying to keep her voice softer, calm. "I just think—"

"Dammit, Jody. I said no!"

Sienna wasn't sure how to respond.

Finally, it was Hope's quiet voice that filled the silence. "That's not Jody, Vivi. It's Sienna."

Vivi's angry face melted away as bewilderment clouded her eyes. Sienna realized she preferred the anger. Her grandmother's gaze passed from Sienna to Hope, appearing so lost, it took all the strength in Sienna's body not to rise and wrap Vivi up in her embrace. To drop her request. To promise that everything would be okay.

"Fine," Vivi said at last. "Set up the appointment, Sienna. I'll go." She walked back into the house leaving Hope and Sienna floundering for answers.

It was several hours later when Sienna made her way to the stable. She and Hope had made an appointment with Sienna's boss for after New Year's. Dr. Spencer assured them he'd do a thorough exam and he agreed that the girls were right to insist

Vivi come in.

Once they'd spoken to the doctor, they called Sterling and Jade to tell them what had happened. All four girls made plans to accompany Vivi to the appointment. Talking to her cousins had gone a long way toward soothing Sienna's concerns, but she still couldn't quite let go of her anxiety.

She hoped Daniel could offer her some sort of solace. He had a way of taking her mind off her worries, either with jokes or sexual innuendoes. Every night, they'd come together in a mad dash, stripping off their clothing and tumbling onto the bed, barely speaking a word. The sex was incredible, but she enjoyed the cuddling that came afterwards just as much. Daniel would hold her as they talked—their conversations little bits of nothing most of the time. Lately, it felt as if he was tempering so many of her rough edges.

After her distressing conversation with Vivi, she hoped to do some forgetting of her own.

She glanced around the stable, disappointed when she found it empty. She hadn't sought Daniel out during the day this week, appreciating their need to be circumspect. But today...she needed him.

"Hey," Sienna cried when strong arms engulfed her from behind. She relaxed within seconds, recognizing Daniel's touch.

"Shh." Daniel's breath tickled her ear. "Walk."

She obeyed his hushed demand for silence, amazed by the instant arousal his touch provoked. He propelled her toward the tack room. The windowless space was small and dark. Once they were inside, Daniel didn't bother to turn on the light. She jerked when she heard the door close behind them, twisting in his arms.

"What are you do—"

Daniel cut off her question with a kiss that not only robbed her words, it stole her air as well.

"No talking or I'll gag you."

Daniel's voice was dark, threatening, hot as hell. God, he'd remembered her capture fantasy. She'd secretly worried she had told him too much about her dark desires that first night because he hadn't mentioned them since.

In the past week, though the sex had been hotter than hell, it had also been fairly straightforward. Usually, he met her outside the back door of her house and walked with her to his trailer. By the time they got to his place, they were too hot and bothered to do much more than tear each other's clothes off and fuck as if their lives depended on it. She'd never felt so much passion, such heart-racing need in her life. The days dragged by at a snail's pace while she waited for the time when she could fall into Daniel's bed again.

"Daniel," she started.

He turned her away from him, dragging her arms behind her back. "You've got the wrong guy. Now be quiet and you won't get hurt."

She shivered with excitement when she felt him wrap something around her wrists. He was tying her up. This was real.

She wasn't about to waste a hot fantasy. Sienna started to struggle. Her sudden spring into motion caught Daniel by surprise, but only for a moment. Then he managed to recapture the arm she'd freed, showing her exactly how strong he was.

Once she was secured, her hands bound behind her back, he spun her around.

"Bad girl," he said in a hushed whisper.

She could hear the voices of several ranch hands passing by outside. The idea that they could be caught at any moment increased her arousal more than she would have thought possible. "Did you lock the door?"

Daniel didn't respond. God. Had he? She couldn't remember hearing the lock *snick* into place, but she hadn't exactly been listening for it. Anyone could walk in.

His hands caught in her hair, tugging it tightly as he drew her closer. "You're mine." Two words had never sounded so threatening...and delicious.

She tried to escape his grip. He would have to earn the right to that claim. "I belong to myself."

"Is that right?"

They spoke softly, their voices hushed so they wouldn't be heard beyond the door. The same couldn't be said of the men speaking outside. A few of the ranch hands were obviously hanging out after a long day's work, chewing the fat—as her father would say. The stable was never a quiet place this time of day. Sienna couldn't believe Daniel was taking such a risk.

"I've captured you. I can do any damn thing to you that I want."

The stable was filled with male laughter. She trembled with anticipation and a healthy dose of fear. Who would have thought those two emotions could be so arousing?

"In fact, I could open that door and invite some of those cowboys to join us."

It was an empty threat. At least...she thought it was.

What did she really know about Daniel's preferences? They'd spent their nights lost in a haze of sexual exploration, but there hadn't been much in the way of pillow talk. None of the usual let's-get-acquainted games that Jade and Sterling had told her were common in new relationships. She and Daniel had gone straight from acquaintances to friends with benefits. She'd purposely avoided delving deeper into his past because she was determined to take her grandmother's advice. This was the new Sienna. The one who took each day as it came.

"How many should I let in? Two? Three? Six?"

She gasped, trying to fill her lungs with air. Would he really share her? Would she let him?

Fuck. Her heart tripled its pace as she considered what it would be like to be taken by so many men at one time. Curiosity warred with true panic. "Daniel. I—"

Her voice seized up. Daniel seemed to take her sudden silence as consent.

"I see." Daniel released his grip, walking toward the door.

Panic set in. "No!" Her refusal came out louder than she intended, but it didn't appear that anyone in the stable heard.

Daniel returned to her and his hands gripped her face between his large palms. Her eyes had begun to adjust to the dim room. She could see relief in his expression. "Good. I don't share."

He didn't need to freaking share. There were times when she felt like *he* was too much man for her. He'd driven her to orgasm after orgasm, night after night.

However, the idea that he would have gone against character to offer her a different fantasy touched her. He'd truly walked to the door with the intention of giving her what he thought she wanted. Had anyone ever cared so much about her desires? Had Josh?

She'd promised Daniel their first night together she wouldn't bring Josh into the bedroom with them. She'd tried very hard to keep that vow, but there were times when it was nearly impossible not to make comparisons. The sum total of her sexual experiences had been exclusively with Josh. He was the yardstick she measured by.

Or had.

Something told her from now on, Daniel was going to be the stick. And she had very little faith anyone else would ever compare.

She tried to escape his grip, while shaking off her memories. She wanted this and she wasn't going to waste a single second thinking about the past. "You can't control me," she taunted. "I'm free, remember? I can sleep with anyone I please."

She heard the rasping of a zipper, then felt Daniel pressing her down, toward the floor. "I told you not to talk. Looks like I'll have to fill that sweet mouth to keep you quiet."

She dropped to her knees far too willingly for a captive. Daniel chuckled at her enthusiasm. "My beautiful slut."

It was a strong word. Sienna began to blast him for it, starting to stand as she did so, but Daniel's strength was irrefutable. He had the power to take whatever he desired and he proved it. With one of his hands, he cupped the back of her neck, holding her in place, while the other guided his cock to her mouth.

"What were you saying about control?" He pushed the mushroom-shaped head between her lips.

God, he was trying to provoke her on purpose, initiating a fight. She tried to rise, but he held her in place, his large palms engulfing her face as he pushed his cock deeper. She truly was captive. The fantasy gave way, mingling with reality, taking her to a place she'd never known.

She tried to shrug off the bindings at her wrists, but her cowboy knew his knots. Try as she may, she wouldn't be released from their hold until he decided it was time.

He continued to thrust his cock into her mouth and soon her struggles for freedom turned to silent demands for more. Her pussy clenched, and she longed for the use of her hands. If only she could touch herself. Two quick strokes on her clit and she'd likely go off like a bottle rocket. She whimpered around Daniel's thick erection—torn between how much she loved his dominance and the temptation to demand he take care of her needs first.

Every night, she'd come to his bed, desperate for his touch.

Every night, she'd become his willing slave, relinquishing every ounce of control into his very capable hands.

It was heady, addictive, overwhelming. An absolute release of power.

Her inner muscles tightened again and she cried out, the intense need painful.

Daniel didn't give in. "Be a good girl and suck my dick, Sienna. Give me what I ask for and I'll make sure you get what you need."

Her brain screamed at her to bite him for being such a cocky male chauvinist pig. Her body refused. She was putty in his hands.

Soon, she became aware of how much she relied on her ability to touch during blowjobs. She'd use her fingers to help her, cupping Daniel's balls, squeezing the base. Without them, she was forced to pay attention to her tongue, her teeth. She closed her lips tighter around him and sucked. She was rewarded by Daniel's low groan.

"God, yeah. Just like that." His words of praise drove her on. She pressed her tongue more firmly against the sensitive spot just beneath the head. His fingers gripped her hair, pulling until her scalp tingled with a pain that besieged her, turning into a pleasure that weaved its way down to her empty pussy.

She sucked harder.

"Fuck." Daniel's tone told her he was close. "Not this way."

His hands reached beneath her arms, tugging her up before he could come. Sienna started to complain. She was dying to taste him. "No. Wait—"

He halted her with a hard, short kiss.

"You're going to finish that blowjob later tonight. But for now, turn around."

She complied without argument, too far gone to consider anything except the fact she needed to obey, needed his cock inside her. Now.

Daniel, the gentlest of souls with the horses and her brothers, turned into a demanding sex god in the bedroom. She never knew what he'd do next, yet she'd never experienced anything at his hands that didn't make her toes curl with incredible delight.

He released the ties around her wrists. Sienna missed them instantly. A disappointed mewl escaped, and Daniel chuckled. "Don't worry. Those ties are going to get plenty more use. I have plans to see you bound spread-eagle on my bed...a few times."

She licked her lips, imagining just how much she enjoyed being at Daniel's mercy. His hands made quick work of the snap and zipper of her jeans. He tugged the denim and her panties down, using his boot to help him tug one leg free from around her shoe. He didn't bother to free himself or her of any more clothing.

"Hey," she heard a male voice call from the stable. "Anybody seen Lennon?"

She giggled, nerves mingling with provocation. Daniel's hand crept around her, covering her mouth. More moisture dampened her pussy. God. She wasn't sure what it said about her, but she loved the way he manhandled her.

She felt the head of his cock graze her opening as he pushed her legs farther apart.

"Fuck." He released her mouth and she felt him rooting around in the dark. She knew what was missing.

"I'm on birth control."

Daniel stopped moving. "Sienna—"

"Fuck me, Daniel. Now." He wasn't the only one capable of making some demands.

He was back in an instant, his cock penetrating her in one rough thrust that made her groan.

"Didn't realize just how loud a lover you are." Daniel's jest would have provoked a laugh if he didn't punctuate it with two deeper, harder passes.

"God," she cried.

His hand returned to her mouth, causing her pussy to tighten.

"Holy shit. Keep doing that and this isn't going to last long." He used his free hand to pinch one of her nipples roughly. Her cunt clamped down again and she barely restrained from coming.

"That's it, Sienna. Be ready for tonight, sweetheart. I'm going to tie you up, gag you, fuck you hard."

She squirmed in his arms, struggling for more. He increased his thrusts. They were back to chest, with very little room to move. It didn't matter. Daniel's rough possession, his hand on her mouth, his whispered dirty words filled every empty, lonely spot inside her.

She trembled as he rubbed her clit. "You're mine. Come for me, Sienna."

Her body splintered, ruptured into a million bright shiny

pieces, putting the sun to shame. She'd never felt so desired, so beautiful, so complete.

Daniel came with her, his come filling her. His arms tightened around her, supporting her with that strength she'd begun to rely on. He'd never let her fall.

Vivi's story about JD flashed through her mind. No. This was different. So different.

Wasn't it?

Neither of them moved for several moments as they waited for their breathing and hearts to slow. Daniel was the first to stir.

He withdrew, fastened his pants, then bent to dress her. Once he had her jeans in place, he gripped her waist and offered her a kiss so sweet, it seemed in direct opposition to the forceful claim he'd just staked.

"Stick around a little while," he said. "You can help me work with that new horse your dad just bought."

Sienna wanted nothing more than to spend the afternoon with Daniel, but without the protection of the condom, she was a bit sticky. "I should probably go inside. Get a shower."

He shook his head. "No. You're staying with me. I like the idea of you walking around with my scent on your skin, my come inside you. I told you, See. You're mine."

His words confused her, thrilled her, scared her. While he'd staked his claim on her body, he'd never alluded to expecting anything more from her.

Maybe they'd been fools to jump into bed without setting up guidelines. This was what came from living day-to-day. The old Sienna would never have let this affair begin without establishing rules.

She started to protest his assertion, but the words wouldn't come. She was happy for the first time in a long time. She wouldn't ruin things by reverting to character.

"I'll stay," she said.

He walked to the door. She was relieved when she watched him unlock it. He'd protected her, even while giving her the illusion of danger. "Where's the key that opens the door from the outside?"

"In my pocket."

She grinned, standing back as he opened the door and looked around. "Coast is clear. Come on."

She followed him to the corral where her dad's new horse stood. "Now," he said, handing her a halter and a rope, "why don't you tell me why you were so upset earlier?"

He'd noticed that? "What?"

"I didn't like that serious expression on your face," he said. "Thought you could use a diversion."

She laughed. "Here's a little FYI for you. You can distract me anytime."

He winked. "I appreciate the permission. And just so you know, I intended to do that anyway. So what's up?"

They worked side-by-side for nearly an hour as she told him about her concerns over Vivi's failing memory. He listened patiently, offering words of comfort and advice, until the heaviness that lingered in her chest lifted completely.

As they washed up, he told her dirty jokes until tears streamed down her face. One week had passed since she'd entered this casual affair with Daniel.

It had been the best week of her life.

Chapter Eight

Daniel smiled as he handed Sienna the Christmas package. He usually sucked at shopping for the holidays, but when he'd spotted the deep green scarf, two things had occurred to him—how pretty the color would be next to Sienna's chestnut hair and chocolate brown eyes and how sexy she'd look with it tying her to his bed.

Sienna grinned as she tore the wrapping paper and lifted the lid. "You really didn't have to get me anything," she said for the tenth time.

"I saw it and thought of you. That's all." She bit her lip until he added, "You can give me my present tonight when you come to the trailer."

"What makes you think I bought you anything?"

"I'm hoping you didn't buy me anything and I can use that guilt you're feeling to get what I really want."

She rolled her eyes. "That transparent, am I?"

He shrugged.

"Well, I do feel guilty. I really screwed up the Christmas gift-giving this year. Got James the wrong size shirt and bought Doug a video game he already has. And now..." She paused. "I didn't get you anything at all. I think I'd like a holiday do-over."

"Good news. You'll get your do-over. It's called next

Christmas." Daniel leaned back on the couch where they were sitting, letting his arm drape along the cushions so he could touch her hair. They were maintaining a proper distance, still trying to keep their affair a secret. At first, Daniel had asked that they lay low. Seth wasn't someone he ever wanted on his bad side.

However, as the weeks passed, he found himself aching to tell the world she was his. The annoying part of that was...she wasn't. Sienna was still clinging tightly to the casual affair idea despite the evidence suggesting that they were well suited. They were never lacking for conversation, enjoyed riding horses together, loved Compass Ranch, and their compatibility in the bedroom was off the charts. So much so he thought maybe he should start taking vitamins and working out so he could keep up with the recently freed sex kitten. She was insatiable, passionate, adventurous and amazing.

Since their rendezvous in the tack room, Sienna had dared him into two more rounds of afternoon delight in that tiny closet as well as one quick roll in the hay...literally, in the barn hayloft.

Less than a month in and he suspected he hadn't touched the tip of the iceberg as far as all the ways he could make love to Miss Sienna Compton.

Love. The word kept sneaking up on him at odd times, taking him unaware. He'd gone into this relationship with the intention of keeping it light, giving Sienna just what she needed and nothing more.

She'd made it clear on too many occasions their sex games were just that—games. She wasn't interested in a boyfriend or a future. His determination to teach her how to live in the moment had come back to bite him in the ass.

"Oh." Sienna pulled the soft scarf from the box. "Daniel. It's beautiful." He'd lured her away from the large family still gathered around the dining room table—even though the meal had ended—to give it to her. They'd spent the morning surrounded by the whole clan again. While Thanksgiving had felt a bit overwhelming as he was still trying to learn names and faces, this time it was easier. He'd established friendships with quite a few of the Comptons. He was touched by their willingness to accept a stranger into their midst and treat him like family.

He leaned closer. "Bring it tonight. I have plans for that scarf. And another gift. One that I didn't think you'd like anyone in your family to stumble on accidentally."

She gave him a wicked grin. "Damn. You're good. And you're totally getting whatever you want tonight."

Daniel sucked in a deep breath, wishing she'd lay off the sexy smiles while her family was sitting in the next room. He'd been flying at half-mast all day, trying to conceal his erection from her mom, aunts, younger cousins and, most especially, her dad. "Dammit, See," he whispered when her gaze lowered to his crotch. She knew exactly what effect she was having on him. Little minx would use it against him.

"Maybe we should try to find somewhere private. I could give you the first part of your gift now." She dragged her hand along the front of his pants. Her too-soft touch was enough. He stiffened up like a pike.

Loud voices alerted them that her family had finally managed to drag themselves away from the table. Sienna moved a few inches away from him on the couch, just as her dad and his brothers, Sawyer, Silas and Sam, entered the room.

"Another present?" Sam asked, spotting the package still on Sienna's lap.

She nodded. "Daniel bought me a scarf."

Daniel tried to look impassive, though he definitely spied curiosity on Seth's face. He shrugged, trying to downplay the gift's significance. "Damn cold winter we're having."

It was a lame reason to buy a gift for the boss's daughter, a woman who supposedly fell into the "just friends" category.

Sienna laughed lightly. "It was a very nice gesture." She started to say more, but her phone beeped. As Sienna pulled it from her pocket, Daniel spotted Josh's face on the screen.

Daniel gritted his teeth.

Sienna's smile dimmed a bit, but she put her present down and rose anyway. "I guess I should take this."

She said, "Merry Christmas, Josh," as she started to leave the living room. "How's Florida?"

"It's great, but I sure do miss Compton Pass and you. Feels weird working on a tan in December. You'd love it here, See. There's a huge pool in the hotel that..."

Sienna hastily left the room before Daniel could hear any more of the conversation. She cast an uncomfortable glance at him over her shoulder.

Daniel's hand clenched in a fist as a wave of pure, unadulterated jealousy rumbled through him. Why the fuck was Josh calling? He thought they were on a goddamn break.

Seth's words mirrored Daniel's thoughts. "Damn. I wish that boy would stop stringing her along."

Daniel agreed, then something in Seth's comment tweaked him. "Has Josh been calling her since Thanksgiving?"

Seth nodded. "Just a few times, but it's enough to put Sienna in a funk for a few hours."

Josh had been calling? Why hadn't Sienna told him that?

Daniel didn't reply, but Seth appeared to be very good at reading faces.

Seth lifted his chin toward the package Sienna had abandoned. "Nice gift. Didn't realize you and Sienna had become such close friends."

Silas glanced at his brother, then Daniel, but he didn't speak. He didn't need to. He was the one brother who intimidated the fuck out of Daniel. Silas was a fair man, but damn if his large stance and dark scowl didn't feel like the blinding, bright lights of an interrogation at times.

Daniel needed to tread lightly. He'd been dreading this conversation with Seth. There was no way in hell he could survive it with all four Compass brothers glowering at him. "She's a nice girl. She's made me feel welcome here." He picked every word with care. While he hoped to eventually come clean about his feelings for Sienna, he wasn't going to discuss them with these men until he'd sorted them out with her. Regardless of his desire to date See, he suspected it wasn't wise to mention he'd been fucking Seth's daughter six ways from Sunday, especially since they'd all just shared Christmas dinner.

Seth leaned back in his chair, but the relaxed posture didn't fool Daniel for a minute. "She's a *very* nice girl. And she's going through a rough patch right now. I'd like to see her avoid sticky entanglements until she sorts out all this shit with Josh. She's still young and inexperienced as far as relationships go. I'd like to see her hang on to that innocence for a while longer. If you catch my drift."

Daniel nodded. Sienna had been inexperienced...a month ago. Now...

Shit. It took all of Daniel's energy simply to school his features. If Seth expected an intelligent response, he was going to be disappointed.

Sawyer broke the awkward silence by chuckling. "Careful there, Seth. You're starting to sound just like Thomas

Kirkland."

Seth shot his brother a dirty look.

"Who's that?" Daniel asked.

"Jody's father. Seth's old boss," Sawyer answered.

When he failed to elaborate on the comparison, Sam continued the conversation. "Thomas spent quite a few years warning Seth to stay away from Jody."

Daniel frowned. "Why?"

Seth sat straighter. "She was a few years younger than me and heading off to college. Thomas was determined she get her degree. I took heed."

Silas laughed. "The fuck you did. You bided your time, I'll give you that, but the second that girl came home from graduation, you kidnapped her ass and tied her to your bed. If I recall correctly, Jody was about the same age Sienna is right now."

Daniel struggled to figure out if Silas was joking. It was impossible to read the man's humor. "Kidnapped her?"

Seth didn't appear to be happy with the direction of their conversation. He'd obviously intended to warn Daniel to stay away from Sienna, but his brothers were turning into Daniel's unexpected allies—whether they realized it or not.

Sawyer leaned forward, happy to share the juicy story with Daniel. "Jody didn't just come home with a diploma. She had a fiancé in tow too. Seth had listened to Thomas' warnings to stay away, but Jody didn't take too kindly to being put off. So she moved on."

Seth crossed his arms. "I'd hardly call Paul moving on."

Daniel tilted his head. "Paul? You mean the Paul that's out there in the kitchen helping the women get dessert ready? The one who's here with Chase? Didn't he realize he was gay back then?"

Seth nodded. "He knew."

Sam picked up the story. "Jody wasn't going down without a fight. She decided to make Seth work to win her affections back."

"So you kidnapped her and tied her to your bed until she fell in love with you?" Daniel had to admit the idea had merit. He didn't like Sienna talking to Josh. He recalled the scarf and his plans for it.

Seth's gaze sharpened. "I wouldn't suggest that course to anyone else. I got lucky. It worked for me. *And* I had her father's blessing to proceed."

Daniel blinked. "Jody's dad knew you were kidnapping her? Forgive me, Seth, but that is one fucked-up way of proposing."

Sawyer and Sam laughed.

Silas shook his head. "Oh Jesus, kid. You ain't heard nothin'. I think Seth's proposal was the least fucked-up of all us Comptons."

Sam was the first to sober up, his face serious and kind as he caught Daniel's eye. He wasn't sure what Sienna's uncle saw, but Daniel was afraid it was too much. Hell, he was pretty sure every single one of the men now realized he was falling for Sienna. "I'll tell you right now, Daniel. Any woman worth having is worth fighting for."

Sam's words drifted back to Daniel off and on throughout the day. Only two months had passed since he'd first laid eyes on Sienna, but given the current state of his heart, it felt like he'd known her forever.

Seth had mentioned Sienna's inexperience, but it seemed

to Daniel that in the committed relationship realm, she was vastly wiser than he was. He'd offered Sienna an easy, no-strings affair because that was as far as his limited experience extended. She'd accepted because that was all she wanted.

How could he convince her to change the rules now? To take a chance with a man she'd only known a short while? A man whose current life ambition was simply to be happy?

He was a washed-up rodeo star turned ranch hand living in a rusty RV, and while Josh was a tool, at least he appeared to have a promising future ahead of him. If he ever managed to graduate, he'd have a degree and a prosperous business. He could give Sienna a big house, financial security, kids.

Daniel rubbed his eyes wearily. All he had to offer was a fun time between the sheets—shits and giggles, slaps and tickles.

Any woman worth having was worth fighting for.

There was no doubt Sienna was worth the fight, but was he the right man to throw the punch?

A light knock sounded. Daniel frowned and glanced at the clock. He'd told Sienna he'd meet her at twelve to escort her back here. It had become his nightly ritual to pick her up for their midnight trysts. He hadn't liked the idea of her traipsing around the ranch alone so late at night. While he'd met and befriended most of the hands, there were still a few men—too fond of their liquor—who might be tempted by the sight of Sienna out alone.

He opened the door. Sienna was bundled in her winter jacket, the green scarf he'd given her wrapped loosely around her neck. "It's only eleven."

She walked in, shrugging off the coat and tossing it on the couch. "The house quieted down early. Guess everyone was worn out from the holiday partying."

"You should have texted me. I would have come to get you."

Sienna rolled her eyes. She'd told him almost nightly she didn't need his escort. Tonight, she let her expression do the talking.

He grinned, but made no move toward her. Sienna frowned, confused by his reticence.

She leaned against his small kitchen counter. "Feel like unwrapping your present?"

There was nothing he desired more, but something held him back. "What did Josh have to say?"

Sienna bit her lip, his question catching her off-guard. "Nothing much. He just wished me a merry Christmas."

He nodded slowly. "Seth said he's called you a few times since Thanksgiving."

"Yeah, so?"

"So why didn't you tell me?"

Sienna fiddled uncomfortably with the edge of her scarf. "Never came up. I didn't think it mattered."

He tried to take a steadying breath. He failed. "It matters."

"Why?"

Because he was fucking in love with her. Because he didn't like her prick of an ex using her—trying to have his cake and eat it too. The bastard asked for a break, but rather than walk away and leave her alone, he kept calling, kept her on an invisible rope Sienna couldn't seem to see. He didn't say any of that. Instead...

"I don't think it's a good idea for you two to keep talking. I thought you were trying to move forward. Find out who you are without him."

The anger he'd seen sparking at his questions faded. "I'm doing that. A few phone calls aren't stopping me." He didn't agree.

She stepped closer. "Are we really going to waste tonight talking about Josh?"

He didn't want to, but it seemed like avoiding the topic wasn't working for them.

Sienna ran her hand along his chest. "You promised me another present."

He remembered the little package he had wrapped and placed on his nightstand. Thoughts of Josh were wiped away as he pictured Sienna wearing her new gifts. Maybe he didn't have a ton of money or a fancy degree to offer, but he knew how to touch her so she shimmered like a lake in the moonlight. For now, it would have to be enough. His cock thickened.

"You already opened one of yours. Now it's my turn to unwrap a gift." Daniel lifted the green scarf from her neck, placing it around his. Then he reached for the hem of her sweater, wasting no time dragging the cashmere away from her body. Soft as the material was, it didn't hold a candle to the delicate texture of her bare skin. He caught sight of her black bra, the lacy little bit of nothing that accentuated her breasts perfectly.

"New?" he asked.

She nodded. "Hope gave it to me. Said she thought you might like it."

"I'll have to remember to thank her."

Sienna giggled. "My cousins love you."

While he knew she meant her words as a compliment, they stung a bit. He wasn't as interested in the love of her cousins as he was in hers. Instead, he pushed the thought away, running his finger along the tops of her breasts.

Sienna inhaled softly. She seemed to enjoy his light touch

as much as his rougher strokes.

"You're leaving the bra on."

She blinked. "I am?"

"Hell yeah. I love the way that looks on you."

She grinned, her hands moving to the button on her jeans. "Then you're in for a treat, because there are matching panties."

He swatted her hands away when she started to unzip her pants. "My present," he reminded her.

He finished the task she'd begun, making short work of her jeans after she kicked off her boots. She was right. The thong that matched her bra was equally deadly to his self-control.

The thin lace of her bra did nothing to hide her pebbled nipples. Daniel leaned forward, cupping her flesh to take a taste. He used the lace between his tongue and her sensitive nub to build her arousal.

Sienna gripped his hair tightly, holding him to her as she silently begged for more. Her breasts were a hot spot for her. A few hard sucks and well-timed nips could drive her to the edge quickly. Daniel was determined that—one day in the future—he'd buy her nipple clamps and play with her breasts until she came. Unfortunately, this was all still too new. Though he tried to draw out each night, squeezing as many exciting experiences in as possible, the truth was she was simply too powerful for him to resist. She'd whimper or touch him a certain way and his restraint would shatter until he had no choice but to fuck her or die.

"Bedroom," he growled.

Sienna led him along the narrow hallway, his gaze glued to the way her thong did nothing to shield her gorgeous ass. He sucked in some much-needed air. He had planned tonight out carefully, until every detail was likely to be etched in his fantasies forever.

He grinned at the irony. He'd convinced Sienna that life could be fun if she was willing to go with the flow, to give up her need to plan everything to the nth degree and let things happen naturally. However, since taking her to his bed, he'd lost that ability himself. She inspired a million fantasies and he was determined to see every single one of them transpire.

Sienna crawled onto the bed before rolling onto her back and beckoning him with the crook of her finger. It would be so easy to join her there. To climb over her body and take her. God knew that was what his cock was voting for.

"Not yet."

She started to sit up when he didn't come closer. He jumped into action. Placing one knee on the bed by her side, he pressed her shoulders back to the mattress before grasping her wrists.

He raised them to the headboard. "Leave them there."

Sienna's breathing accelerated, her chest rising and falling more rapidly.

Taking the scarf he'd given her from his neck, he used it to bind her hands together and then to his bed. Sienna didn't fight him as she had in the tack room. This wasn't a capture. This was a claiming, pure and simple. And she was his warm, willing slave.

Despite her desire to be bound, Sienna couldn't resist testing the waters. She tugged against the scarf, but it didn't give.

"This is what happens when you play with a rodeo cowboy," he taunted. "Knots are my specialty." Reaching down, he stripped off her tiny thong, tossing it aside.

She swallowed heavily, but her face didn't show fear.

Instead, it was the picture of unbridled lust. "Take off your clothes."

He shook his head. There was something heady, something hot about having Sienna bound, naked in his bed while he remained fully clothed. "I realize old habits die hard, but you always tend to forget—you're not calling the shots, Sienna. I am."

She licked her lips. "Then call them faster. I'm dying here."

He chuckled at her breathless demand. She may accept his commands in the bedroom, but she'd never truly be ruled by any man. She was too strong, too opinionated. Hell, she had too much Compton blood running through her veins. Daniel recalled Sawyer's story, considered how Seth had captured his own dark-haired bride this way. How much was Sienna like her mother?

Daniel reached toward the nightstand, Sienna's gaze following his hand. If she'd seen the small wrapped package there when she entered his room, she didn't mention it.

He glanced at her bound hands and gave her a rueful grin. "Looks like I'll have to open this gift for you."

Her eyes took in his progress, widening when he removed the lid and revealed the vibrator inside.

The tips of her lips lifted in a crooked grin. "I already have one of those. I was pretty happy to replace it with you."

He removed the vibrator from the box. He'd taken it from its original packaging and washed it earlier in the day. He knew himself well enough to know he'd never have the patience for that simple act tonight. He'd been correct.

Daniel grabbed lube from his nightstand. "This isn't a replacement," he explained as he knelt between her outspread legs. "It's an addition."

She blinked rapidly, her brow creasing with curiosity. He didn't bother to say more. Actions spoke louder anyway.

He squeezed a healthy dollop of lube on his finger and pressed it to her anus. Sienna gasped. They'd toyed with anal play since the very first night, but Daniel had never extended the exploration beyond a single digit. Tonight, they were going to expand on that.

He worked the lube into her tight opening. Removing his finger, he placed the nozzle of the lube against her ass, adding even more sticky gel. This time, it wasn't one finger entering her, it was two.

Sienna groaned softly, a perfect mixture of pleasure and pain. He'd grown accustomed to all her sex sounds. He knew when she needed a break…and when she wanted more. Her hips rose from the mattress, urging him to go deeper.

He accepted the invitation and pushed his fingers inside her…repeatedly.

When he decided she was ready, he removed them. Spreading lube on the vibrator, he slowly worked it into her ass. It was thicker than his two fingers and definitely longer. Even so, it was much smaller than his cock. They'd add that adventure another time.

Tonight he had a different plan. Once the vibrator was fully lodged inside, he turned it on its slowest speed. Sienna's hips jerked, her hands suddenly fighting against her bondage in earnest.

"God, Daniel. So good." Then she added, "Not enough."

She continued to thrash, her body seeking the extra stimulus it needed. While the vibrator got her motor revving, it wasn't kicking her into overdrive. He let the pressure build, forced himself to count to ten, then twenty as her back arched and she yelled her wicked demands.

"Fuck me. Oh God. Hurts so much. Need..."

Her face flushed with exertion as a thin sheen of sweat covered her creamy skin. He recalled how frozen she'd seemed when he'd first arrived. He had to admit there was nothing more beautiful than watching Sienna's sexual thaw.

Soon her cries dissolved to one word. Just one. "Please."

He opened his pants, shoving them to his knees. It was all he had time for. Once again, he'd thrown himself on his own knife. He'd planned to drive Sienna wild, but he'd taken himself down as well.

He shoved his cock into her wet pussy with a thrust that was almost brutal in its intensity. He needed her too fucking bad. The vibrator in her ass had him clenching his teeth, praying not to come.

Too much. With her, it was always too much. Too incredible.

Sienna grunted at his rough entry, but offered no complaint. Her gaze pierced his. "Please," she repeated.

He was a goner. Fuck it. Reaching down, he cranked the vibrator up, skipping the middle speed, shooting it straight to high.

Sienna arched, her body taking on a life and a strength of its own. Her pussy clamped down on his cock until he saw stars behind his eyes. Pure animalistic need clawed its way to the surface. He pounded into her, his usual control and finesse gone.

"Jesus, See." The words were dragged from his chest, sounding more like a growl than true words.

He grasped her breast, his finger and thumb rolling the taut peak harder through her bra. And harder. She heaved against him once more. Her closed eyes clenched tight, her breath thready, harsh.

Daniel continued to move inside, their pelvises slapping out an uneven rhythm. Finally, there was no going back.

"See." Her name was a prayer, a promise, a plea. "Sienna."

Strong jets of come filled her, mixing with her own hot liquid. His name on her lips signaled she was with him as she cried out her sweet release. They were together.

She may be his captive, but there was nothing docile about his lover. She lifted her head. And bit his shoulder.

His gaze flew to her face, catching her wicked grin. "Mine," she whispered.

His eyes narrowed. She had no idea.

Reaching up, he released her hands, rubbing her shoulders at her slight wince. He pulled the vibrator out of her ass, turned it off and tossed it to the floor with her panties. All of his movements were clumsy, heavy. Daniel felt like he was trapped in quicksand up to his neck.

He collapsed next to her and for several long minutes, the only sound in the room was that of their labored inhalations. He knew the second hers turned from wakefulness to sleep.

Lifting his head, he gently pushed a stray tendril of hair away from her eyes as he soaked up the peaceful expression on her face.

She said she hadn't gotten him a gift. She was wrong.

She was exactly what he wanted, even if he hadn't realized it until this moment.

Now he had a true goal.

A future. A forever.

"Goodnight, Sienna," he whispered.

Chapter Nine

Daniel sat at Spurs, drinking a beer. He was trying to talk himself out of flying to Florida to beat the fuck out of a man he'd met only one time but who was making his life a living hell. He'd invited Sienna out for a drink. Unfortunately, several other ranch hands had been around when he'd asked and what he'd intended to be their first formal date had turned into a big group of friends, playing pool and getting rowdy.

He'd hoped after Christmas she was ready to turn a corner, to give up on Josh altogether. Now she was standing outside in the cold winter wind, talking to the prick on the phone while he sat inside nursing a warm PBR.

"What's up?" Jade leaned against the counter across from him.

"Working tonight?"

She nodded. "Yep. My shift just started. You're stuck with me until close. Why aren't you over there with the other hands?"

"Just spent all damn day with them. Needed some quiet time."

Jade nodded, her eyes filled with mischief. "So obviously you decided to come to a rowdy redneck bar on the busiest night of the week. Ah, I love the peace and quiet and tranquility of this place." The sound of glass breaking as a waitress dropped a tray full of beer bottles almost drowned out the last part of her comment."

He grinned. Of all Sienna's cousins, he liked Jade the best. She spoke his language—sarcasm. "I invited Sienna to come out with me. Next thing I know, seven other yahoos added their names to the guest list."

"Sienna's here?" Jade peered around at the growing crowd of partiers. She hadn't been lying—the place was packed. "Damn. I can never get her to go out with me. Where is she?"

He gestured over his shoulder with his thumb. "She's out front. Got a phone call."

An understanding look entered Jade's eyes. "Ah. Josh must have sensed she was having fun and decided to ruin it for her."

He grimaced. "Yeah."

"I told her to block his number."

Daniel nodded. "That's a good idea. I can't understand why she still talks to him after that stupid *I need a break* bullshit at Thanksgiving."

Another patron at the bar caught Jade's eye. She nodded at the unspoken request and started pouring two beers from the tap. "He was pretty clever in the way he worded it. Said he needed some time apart, not that he wanted to break up. He pretended like this separation would be good for both of them and then he promised to come back and play by her rules for as long as they both shall live." She placed air quotes around the last part of her comment.

"Calling her every fucking other day isn't what I consider taking a break."

Jade placed the two beers in front of the guy next to him and took the money the man offered. "I agree. I assume one of two things is going on. First of all, maybe Josh has discovered that the grass is not greener. He was pretty lucky to land Sienna in the first place. She's bright and funny and strong. Josh is more or less the opposite of that. He's always been quiet, a bit shy, too serious. The only time he really shines, really stands out, is when he's with her. Maybe he's realized that he had a good thing all along."

Daniel could definitely buy that idea. He hadn't spoken more than ten words to Josh over Thanksgiving. Mainly because he'd decided from the get-go that he hated the prick. But Jade was right. He hadn't noticed much personality in the other man. "What's the other thing? The other reason why he could be calling all the time?"

Jade frowned. "While he's out there sowing his wild oats, he doesn't want her doing the same."

Daniel had come to that same conclusion two days ago, when he first discovered Josh was calling. "You mean he pretended that this break was for both of them when really it's just for him. Yeah, that's what I was thinking too."

Jade wiped the counter, refilled a couple empty bowls with peanuts. "I hope that reason is wrong, because if I find out he's trying to fuck my cousin over, I will personally beat the shit out of him."

His hand clenched. Jade wasn't going to have to make good on that promise because he intended to get there first. There wasn't going to be much of Josh left by the time he finished with him. Daniel needed to cool off. He took a swallow of the beer and winced. Tasted like piss.

"Here, you can't drink that." Jade dumped his beer in the sink, grabbed a fresh frosty mug and poured him a new one. "On the house."

"What for?"

She grinned. "Because I think you're going to need it." She

nodded toward the entrance. Sienna was making her way to the bar and she seemed upset.

Jade walked away as soon as Sienna reached him. He'd managed to save a stool next to him. "Take a load off," he said, pointing to it.

"Thanks."

"Want a beer?"

She nodded, then tried to get Jade's attention. "I'll have my regular," she called out. Jade raised her hand to indicate that she'd heard.

"Sorry about that." Sienna sat down.

Daniel considered her apology. He'd never been the sort of man to hang back, to give a woman space. His mother used to say she pitied the woman who finally captured his heart because she'd never have a moment's peace. When he saw something he wanted, he went after it with a single-minded determination. The only reason he never took her words as an insult was because she'd go on to blame his father for his rather forceful ways, but his mom's eyes were always soft and happy as she looked at her beloved husband.

He'd seen that same expression when Jody gazed at Seth. He'd even caught it at Christmas when Lucy batted Silas' hand away as he playfully pinched her ass. She'd been complaining about the extra pounds she'd picked up over the last few years. Silas had told her it just gave him more to grab on to. There'd been no doubt that while Lucy wasn't happy with the weight, Silas would never see her as anything less than completely beautiful.

For a month Daniel had given Sienna the free and easy side of himself, played the casual lover, entertaining her fantasies. He'd done it because he thought that was what she'd needed. Now...well, the leash he was wearing was starting to chafe.

"Let me guess. That was Josh."

She nodded. "He's drunk."

"He called to tell you that?"

Sienna laughed. "No. He called to tell me he loved me."

Motherfucker.

Daniel forced himself to take a drink of his beer. It was that or lose his cool. A lot of his current situation was his own fault. He'd let Sienna think he was okay with no strings.

"Is that so?"

She toyed with the label on the bottle of beer Jade had placed in front of her. "Yeah, but the whole time we were talking, all I could think about was..." Her voice drifted away, but Daniel needed to hear the rest.

"Was what?"

"I can't remember the last time he said that to me."

Daniel struggled for an answer that would convince her to give up on Josh once and for all. He wasn't going down without a fight.

Sienna saved him from having to find the right words. "Don't you think it's pretty sad that he can only say those words when he's wasted?"

"Yeah. I think the guy's a jackass, but I've said that before."

"The truth is, he's not. He was right to ask for this break. I didn't think so at first, but obviously Josh saw something I was too blind to recognize and, by asking for this distance, he's really just trying to fix the problem."

Daniel's chest ached. He didn't like where this conversation was heading. "What problem?"

"That even though we're technically adults, we were both actually just silly, inexperienced kids, clinging to a dream we'd concocted when we were too young to make those kind of decisions."

"Do you know what you want now?"

She leaned closer. "I think so. It's weird to admit it, but suggesting this time apart may be the most mature thing Josh has ever done in his life."

Daniel wanted to ignore the admiration in her voice. Though she'd been hurt by her boyfriend and aggravated by his drunk phone call, she still harbored feelings for the man.

She took a long sip of her beer. "You know what?"

"What?"

"I'm sick of talking about Josh. I'm tired of worrying about the future, of wondering what the hell's going on inside his head...and my head. I'm fucking done with all of it. We're here to have fun. Let's do it."

He grinned, though the happiness wasn't sincere. Clearly he had more work to do if he hoped to erase Josh from her mind—and her heart—once and for all. "Dance with me."

She hopped up quickly. He wasn't fool enough to think she'd completely shut Josh out of her mind. He could see a shadow in her eyes that told him she was still upset. It didn't matter. The kid gloves came off tonight. He was about to take ownership of Sienna Compton's heart.

Sienna reached for Daniel's hand, letting him lead them to the crowded dance floor. An old country song, "Honey Bee", started to play. It was one she'd heard her dad sing—badly—to her mom many times when she was a little girl. The words were funny and sweet and silly. Though she'd only been young, she remembered how she and her mom had giggled when Dad danced them around the living room, calling them his honeysuckles.

Daniel took her hands, spinning her around. Damn. He was a smooth dancer. Weeks had passed as she tried to find something the sexy cowboy didn't do well. So far, she hadn't found a single thing.

He drew her closer, the two of them swaying to the beat. Their close proximity brought her in direct contact with one of the things she'd decided she liked best about him. She pressed against his hard cock, her gaze lifting.

"Really, cowboy?"

He chuckled as he grasped her hips, holding her tighter to him. "Sweetheart, if you're around, he's around. It's something I'm learning to live with."

She blushed at his compliment. Weeks spent in his bed hadn't alleviated her need for sex one little bit. If anything, she'd become a raging mass of hormones, walking around in a constant state of arousal.

So much for slaking her needs and moving on. Had there actually been a time in her life when she thought a couple quick tumbles with Josh over the holidays would be enough to soothe her? The sad fact was, it probably would have scratched the itch and she wouldn't have even realized what she was missing. She'd never experienced the same passion for Josh that she felt for Daniel.

The music ended, an upbeat song filling the room.

Daniel bent closer. "You wanna play pool?"

She glanced over her shoulder and discovered most of the Compass ranch hands hanging out around the table. She shook her head. She'd been disappointed when a bunch of the guys had decided to come along with them. Though she didn't think Daniel had intended his invitation as a date, she'd sort of liked the idea of the two of them going out somewhere together.

Alone. In public.

"There's a corner booth over there that's empty." Daniel pointed. "How about I buy you a beer?"

She smiled. "I'd like that."

They claimed the tiny booth. It was tucked away between two larger tables. Sienna wondered if it had been tossed there as an afterthought. Or as a private spot for lovers.

Daniel waved for the waitress to bring them a couple of beers. His arm rested against the back of the cushion and it felt too inviting for her not to wiggle closer. He grinned when her knee brushed his beneath the table, then he wrapped his arm around her shoulder and dragged her over until she was tucked tight to his side. "You smell delicious. Coconut?"

She wondered how she'd ever manage to keep her hands to herself until they made their way back to his place. "Must be my body wash. I like it because it makes me think of summer and sunshine. Helps me pretend it's not freezing outside."

He shrugged. "Has it been cold this winter?" His fingers began to caress the back of her neck. "I hadn't noticed."

"You keep that up and I'm going to straddle you in this booth right here and right now. I'm just going to say to hell with the crowd, my dad, your job and ride you hard."

He groaned, then reached down to adjust his jeans. "Dammit, See. I was hoping we could sit here and talk. Problem is, if you're within fifty feet of me, all I can think about is touching you."

"Talk about what?" she asked.

"I thought it might be nice if we spent a little time getting acquainted with one another."

She tried to ignore the extra skip in her heart, tried not to read too much into his words. He'd never acted like he intended to be more than a casual lover, someone to help her kill the hours between sunset and sunrise. "Why?"

"Do I need a reason?"

Did he? No. And she was a fool to fight what she wanted too. She shook her head. "Actually, I feel like you know me a hell of a lot better than I know you. I've sort of spent weeks monopolizing the conversations with all the Josh bullshit. So fair is fair. Tell me about your last girlfriend."

Daniel didn't balk at her request. Now that she thought about it, there wasn't anything he hadn't shared with her willingly. Though she knew he didn't like to talk about his injuries or his brother's death, he'd told her about them, given her that tiny peek inside. After watching him the past few months on the ranch, she noticed he didn't open up that way with anyone else.

"Last girlfriend. Let me see." His brow creased, and she sensed he was actually thinking about it.

"You don't remember?"

He'd started to take a sip of his beer, but he put the bottle down again. "Well, I assume when you say girlfriend, you don't mean women I've slept with."

A tiny spark of jealousy flared before she could tamp it down. "No. I don't need a list of your past lovers. Thanks anyway."

He chuckled. "Now, don't get your feathers all ruffled. It's not like there were that many." He stressed the word *that* just enough to jerk her chain again.

His grin grew when she scowled. "Just answer my damn question."

"Fine. My last—and only—girlfriend was Jessie. We went out our senior year in high school."

"High school? You haven't dated anyone since then?"

He shook his head. "Why do you sound so surprised? Not to criticize or anything, but didn't you just stop seeing your high school sweetheart?"

She crossed her arms. "We're talking about you. Not me. So what made Jessie so special?"

He shrugged. "She was pretty. We were in a bunch of the same classes. She let me fuck her."

"Ug. Seriously? These were the deciding factors that made her your first—and only—girlfriend?"

"I was seventeen years old, See. Sorry to say, sex was a pretty big deal back then."

Her gaze drifted lower, her eyebrows lifting to indicate that fact didn't seem to have changed much.

He grasped her hand and directed it to his lap, pressing her palm against his denim-covered erection. "You don't have to be shy," he teased.

"I thought we were talking." She didn't bother to move her hand away even though Daniel had released her.

"Don't see any reason why we can't do both." The arm wrapped around her tightened.

"Were you close? In love?"

Daniel considered her questions. "We were kids. I walked her to class so I could sneak kisses in the hallway. We went out on the weekends, parked in the woods so we could have sex in my backseat. I'm sure I thought I loved her at the time. Maybe I really did."

"Why did you and Jessie break up?"

"We graduated. She was going off to college and I was heading West." His finger lightly traced the shell of her ear. She tried to ignore the pressure building in her pussy.

"Were you sad?"

He tilted his head. "Probably. For a little while. She was a nice girl. We got along. It just wasn't our time."

"What about now? There's nothing stopping you from going home and contacting her." Sienna cursed herself for the suggestion. She hated the thought of him leaving Compton Pass.

He reached over with his free hand, lifting her leg to place it over one of his. She should have protested. She was too open, unable to squeeze her legs together for that tiny bit of relief.

"She got married about a year ago, around the same time as my accident. I'd actually planned to go home for the wedding, but life got in the way again."

He'd kept his hand on her knee, but as he spoke, it drifted higher on her thigh. What the hell was he going to do? She'd foolishly worn jeans. Tight jeans. From now on, it was nothing but skirts for her.

"So the two of you are still friends?"

He nodded. "I guess you could say that. Couple emails a year, occasional phone call to catch up. That's it. I haven't seen her since the day I hopped on the plane and headed to Denver seven years ago."

She turned her head to glance around the crowded bar. While the booth was secluded, there was no hiding the fact that she was practically sitting in Daniel's lap.

"Look at me, See."

Her gaze returned to his handsome face. Sometimes at night, when he slept, she'd study his features, trying to figure out what it was that made him so fucking hot. There was a slight crook in his nose that indicated it had been broken once. Hell, maybe more than once. There was a razor-thin scar above his left eyebrow. His jaw was chiseled to the extent that it was almost too sharp, too pointed. His beard grew fast. Though she knew he shaved every morning, right now, his five-o'clock shadow was thick and black. And his eyes were dark, so dark she sometimes struggled to find his pupils amidst the deep brown.

Yet, somehow, when all those features were put together, the result was Daniel. And he—quite simply—took her breath away.

He was ready to leave, anxious to drag them out of here, to find somewhere private. She could see it in his eyes. It was hunger. Pure and simple.

"Is there anything else you would like to know?"

Unfortunately, there was. While she wanted nothing more than to escape to the Neverland of his bed, to shut out the world for another night, there was still one question burning in her mind. "Why hasn't there been anyone else?"

"Time has a funny habit of creeping away. I've spent years, traveling around, never finding a place to put down roots. To try my hand at a real relationship."

It was ironic when she considered it. Sienna had never wanted to be anything other than an adult. She'd tried to escape all the childish things in her rush to be settled. All of her attempts had failed. She was as inexperienced as Daniel. "Now that I think of it, I've never tried that mature relationship thing either."

He tilted his head, studied her face for just a moment. "No," he said at last. "I don't think you have."

His hand stopped moving on her leg, the conversation distracting them both. She was tired of games. Sick of pretending.

"I hear there's a New Year's Dance at the fire hall."

Sienna nodded, surprised by Daniel's abrupt change of subject. "Yeah. Vivi and Mom are on the planning committee. It's all they talk about these days."

"Go with me." It was so like him. He never asked. Just demanded. She told herself she only let him get away with his imperiousness in the bedroom because it turned her on. Truth was it was fucking hot everywhere.

Still, she didn't believe in making things too easy. "Is that a request?"

He shook his head. "No. I'm not taking a chance that you'll refuse."

She laughed. "So what is this? A date?"

"Yeah, Sienna. A date. I'd like to go out with you."

Her heart pounded hard at his request as a tiny nugget of fear crept in. Dating wasn't part of this. She was supposed to be going with the flow, not making more of those cursed future plans. Hell, she hadn't fully shed the last boyfriend. Was she really ready to invite a new guy into her fucked-up life?

"When's the last time you had a quickie in the front seat of a truck?"

Sienna laughed at his unexpected question. He always knew how to take her off-guard, surprise her. "Um. Never?"

Daniel reared back. "Seriously?"

"Josh has never driven a truck."

Daniel grasped her hand, pulling her from the booth. "Well, you're in luck. Because I am in possession of the ranch truck tonight. Spotted a little lane off the main highway on our way here. What do you say we refuse to grow up one more night?"

"How do we do that?"

"You and me are going to go parking."

An hour later, Sienna lay on her back with her head resting in Daniel's lap. The steamy heat of sex fogged up the windows of the truck, but she wasn't interested in seeing what was outside. She stared at Daniel's face, his eyes closed, his head pressed against the back of the seat.

Once again, he'd wiped away all of her inhibitions, anxieties, everything. When she was in his arms, the world disappeared.

Until tonight that release carried over, kept her going, made her strong.

Until tonight...

Now as she lay gazing at his peaceful face she could only think of one thing.

She'd forgotten the rules of spontaneity and kicked the concept of going with the flow to the curb.

She'd done something she'd never done before.

Jumped from the safety of the reliable frying pan straight into the raging, uncontrollable fire. There was no way she wasn't going to get burned now.

Chapter Ten

Daniel watched Mark Parker tug Sienna into his arms as they danced way too close for his comfort. His temper had been on a slow burn all night, but jealousy was seriously kicking in now, adding fuel to the flames. He stood near the edge of the dance floor, forcing air into his lungs. It wouldn't do for him to march over to the couple, drag Mark away from Sienna and punch the guy's lights out.

For one thing, he and Sienna weren't a couple. Though they'd come to the dance together, he'd heard her tell more than a few people they were just there as friends. When Daniel called her on it, she said it was to protect his job. Fuck his job. He'd stuck by the decision to remain silent about their affair more for her than for him. Seth wouldn't fire him for his affair with Sienna. While his boss might not be thrilled, Daniel knew Seth well enough to realize he was fair, a straight shooter. Her father would probably issue a warning, threaten to take a slice out of Daniel's hide if he hurt Sienna. It wouldn't matter because Daniel had no intention of hurting Sienna. Not now. Not ever.

No. There was something else driving her desire to keep him a secret. And he aimed to find out what it was. That was…if he could get within ten feet of her.

Unfortunately, more than a few of the young bucks at the dance had taken notice of a very sexy, very free Sienna, and the sharks had started to circle. No doubt Mark had caught wind of Sienna's "Daniel and I are just friends" bullshit and felt safe to issue his invitation to dance.

What the fuck was she doing? Daniel had made it clear at Spurs this was going to be a date. His jaw tightened. He knew what he'd done. He'd scared her off. For a second, at the table, he thought he'd spotted a flash of panic when he dropped his guard and asked her to be his date tonight. Rather than address the concern, he'd tried to brush it aside, dragging her out to the truck and reverting to form. He'd been a dumbass, thinking he could fuck away her fears.

Now Sienna was running scared. If he could keep his shit together, he'd pull her aside and they'd find a way to work this out...without bloodshed. Mark's hands drifted lower on Sienna's ass.

Fuck it. No, they couldn't.

Daniel had only taken two steps onto the dance floor when Sterling blocked his path. "Easy there, cowboy."

He shook his head. "Get out of my way, Sterling."

"No. I think you need to take a deep breath. Maybe go outside for some fresh air. Think about what you're about to do."

He tried to play off his anger, but Sterling was too savvy to be fooled. "There's nothing wrong with what I'm about to do."

"Oh yeah? Tell me what you're planning."

He gestured to Sienna and her dance partner. "I'm going to go over there and break Mark Parker's neck."

Sterling grinned. "Yeah. That's what I thought. I'm not going to let you."

"Why not?"

"Because you're too close to succeeding with See to fuck it

all up now."

It was the only thing Sterling could have said that would have stopped him. "I'm close?"

"Yeah. You are. So dance with me." Sterling lifted her arms, making it impossible for Daniel to refuse.

He accepted her invitation and led her out onto the floor. "How do you figure I'm winning Sienna over? She's danced with three different guys tonight and flirted with at least half a dozen more."

Sterling glanced over at her cousin briefly, then lifted her gaze to him. "She's in freak-out mode."

"What the hell does that mean?"

"I can only guess you got too close, so now she's initiating a full-out retreat. Jade said you two seemed pretty chummy the other night at Spurs. And you showed up here together."

Daniel grimaced. "She's been avoiding me since we walked in the door."

Sterling nodded. "So I noticed. You're in love with her, aren't you?"

It was the first time anyone had come straight out and asked the question. "Yeah. I am."

"I think she's starting to feel the same way about you."

Daniel glanced over in time to see Sienna laugh at something Mark said, her hands clinging to the other man's shoulders a bit too tightly. "I can see that."

His tone was pure sarcasm, but Sterling didn't take offense. "We've spent years telling Sienna she should date other guys, not to settle for her first love. Now she's taken our advice, but she's falling for the second man. If one guy wasn't enough, what makes two the magic number?"

He shrugged. Sterling's comment sounded logical in his

head, but his heart wasn't interested. "I have no idea what makes it right. It just is."

Sterling paused, studying his face. He wasn't sure what she saw written there, but she dropped her arms. "Okay. So I was wrong. You should go with your instincts."

He wasn't sure what to make of that. His impulse had been to beat the hell out of the guy Sienna was dancing with. Surely her cousin didn't intend for him to do that. Fortunately, the song ended.

Sienna glanced around the room, smiling when she found him. He let the fact that she was looking for him soothe his anger.

Sterling excused herself as Sienna approached.

"Hey," she said. "It's almost midnight. You having fun?"

He nodded stiffly, struggling to find his voice. His temper was too close to the edge. He tried to count to ten, tried to take Sterling's words to heart. Both things failed when Sienna pointed out a blonde in the corner, suggesting that he ask her to dance.

It was the last straw.

"Come with me." He wrapped his arm around her waist tightly, despite her desire to shrug him off.

"Daniel," she said in a hushed, annoyed tone. "Let go of me."

"No." He continued to propel her forward until they reached the hallway. There was a coat closet on the left, a women's bathroom on the right. It was too close to midnight. Too many of the older people would be searching for their coats, ready to take their leave, and there was another bathroom. It made the decision easy. He needed time.

Spying a broken, old-fashioned drinking fountain, he

reached for the Out of Order sign taped to the front. Change came slowly to places like Compton Pass. The fire hall had been built well over fifty years ago and was badly in need of an overhaul.

He pushed her toward the bathroom and slapped the sign on the door. Luckily, the tape was still sticky. It opened as Hope emerged, her gaze widening when she spotted Daniel and Sienna.

Daniel pointed down the hall. "Direct people to the other bathroom, Hope."

Hope's gaze took in the sign, then she nodded.

"What the f—" Sienna didn't have time to finish her statement as he shoved her inside. The last thing he saw before he closed and locked the door was Hope's astonished look dissolving as an amused smile crept to her lips.

"What the hell are you doing?" She started to push by him, intent on leaving. He pressed her back until her thighs hit the sink.

"I'm having a hard time keeping track of my date tonight. Decided it might be easier if I kept her in a contained place."

She glowered at him. "I'm not a fucking dog you can put in a cage. Let go of me."

"No."

She waited for him to elaborate, to say more. He didn't.

"God dammit, Daniel. You have no right to act like—"

"Don't," he interrupted. "Don't say anything else." He was teetering on the edge of a cliff as it was. One push from her and he'd make damn sure they both went tumbling into the abyss.

"What's wrong with you?" Her voice was quieter, confused. If he wasn't mistaken, there was a bit of fear mixed in as well.

She needed to be afraid. Deserved to feel the pulse-pounding terror that was coursing through his own veins right now.

He gripped her shoulders and turned her away from him. Forced her gaze to the mirror in front of them. "You, Sienna. You're what's wrong with me."

She winced.

"You're also what's right with me."

Her eyes closed, sadness creeping onto her face. "No. Daniel. Please. Please don't say anything else."

Jesus. She was tearing his guts out. He could hate her just as easily as he loved her right now, but he could see she was taking no pleasure in any of this. She was in pain too. He'd vowed to erase Josh from her mind. Promised her sex without strings. Fun without commitment.

It wasn't her fault he'd changed his mind.

Truth was, she made him long for things he'd never wanted before. Roots, a home without wheels, love. He'd been a drifter and a loner for so long, he'd convinced himself it was enough. Maybe he and Sienna were more alike than they realized. They'd spent years lying to themselves and others about their true desires.

He was tired of the lies. But Sienna...she wasn't ready to let go yet.

"Fine," he said at last.

Sienna's eyes lifted, her gaze finding his in the reflection.

"Nothing changes, Sienna. You will come to my trailer every night. You will sleep in my arms. And you will find me if you ever need me. No matter what it's for—sex, a laugh, to talk. Hell, I don't care if you just need someone to sit and be quiet with. I'm the man who will give you all of that."

And then he took a chance and added the two words that

truly mattered. "Only me."

She never looked away as he issued his demands. He wouldn't change their status, wouldn't force her into calling this what it was. But she was going to make those concessions.

"Agree?"

She nodded.

"Say it. Out loud."

"I agree," she whispered.

He pressed on her shoulders, forcing her to lean forward. She didn't resist. She continued until her elbows rested on the rim of the sink.

The position gave him a bird's eye view of her cleavage, her breasts spilling out of the top of her tight blouse. He reached beneath her, cupping the flesh roughly. A soft moan escaped Sienna's lips. Her nipples peaked as he pinched them, despite the clothing in his way.

He should walk away right now. Should get the hell out of here and calm down. His emotions were raw, his gut ached. He'd never be able to take her gently. Never.

"Don't leave."

He jerked. Surprised.

She didn't lower her eyes, didn't offer him the chance to escape. "Don't leave."

"Sienna—" His voice broke on her name.

"Please."

Fuck. It was the one word he'd never been able to resist from her. Regardless, he owed her an explanation. A warning.

"I can't..." he started. The words wouldn't come.

"I don't care. Don't go."

He lifted her skirt and fought back the wave of

lightheadedness that attacked when he caught sight of her thong.

He lifted his hand and slapped her bare ass cheek. Sienna started to rise, but he placed his hand on her neck and held her down. Her retreat wasn't based on fear or revulsion. He'd seen it in her face. She was aroused. The leash slipped, fell away.

He spanked her again. And then again.

Soon Sienna began to anticipate his strikes, tried to move into them, rather than away. Her thighs glistened with her arousal as she trembled with need.

She groaned as he painted her ass pink, then red. "More," she pleaded.

Shoving her legs apart, he pulled the thin string of her thong to the side and drove two fingers into her hot pussy. She reared up, her hair falling across her face as she fought for breath, for release.

Daniel didn't temper his movements, didn't hold back as he took her hard. Removing his fingers, he used her body's juices to his ease his way into her ass. She moaned when he pressed the same two fingers deep inside the tight portal.

He needed her to understand. Maybe she couldn't hear the words yet, but she would know by his actions, he would possess her, every part of her—body, soul, heart. He'd give her time to adjust to that, but he wouldn't halt the pursuit, wouldn't wait patiently on the sidelines.

He reached beneath her, shoved his free hand under her thong and found her clit. He rubbed the sensitive nub quickly. She was soaking wet, her body making it far too easy. "Come, Sienna."

She splintered in his arms, but he didn't release her. He continued to fuck her ass with his fingers and stroke her clit until she tumbled again. Sweat gathered at her brow as her fists clenched. "Too much. God, Daniel."

It wasn't. It would never be enough. Dragging his fingers from her body, he reached for her blouse. Releasing the top two buttons, he reached into her bra and pulled her breasts free of the constricting lace. Her bent position, as well as the shirt and bra, framed her breasts perfectly. He cupped the flesh and squeezed.

She moaned, urging him on. He rolled her nipples between his fingers, teasing the taut nubs until they were large, hard peaks. He longed to suck them into his mouth, but he wasn't willing to turn her around and lose the sight of her in the mirror.

Her face flushed. Her hair was a delicious mess, a sienna waterfall. He reached for the soft tresses, drawing them away from her face. Gathering the thick mass in his hand, he wrapped it around his palm, allowing the tension to grow slowly, twist by twist until he pulled her head back.

He swallowed heavily. "Do you see yourself?"

Could she? See how beautiful she was? How perfectly they fit together?

He hastily unfastened his pants and withdrew his cock.

"Yes," she hissed.

Daniel placed the head at her opening, then froze. "Now look at me, Sienna."

Her gaze met his in the mirror once more.

"Do you see?" he asked as he pressed inside. Her eyes held his as he filled her. They never wavered until he was lodged completely within her.

He ached to say the words. Three words. He couldn't deny they were there. That he felt them. But she wasn't ready.

He retreated, then returned. Retreated. Returned. His

thrusts weren't gentle. They weren't easy. He released her hair and gripped her hips, pulling her back to meet him.

Sienna's hands covered his, adding her own force to this incredible merging. Two bodies becoming one. Her fingers tightened, her nails scraping along the skin on his hands, red welts appearing. While he intended to leave his mark tonight, it was clear she wouldn't be the only one wearing the memory.

He moved faster, while trying to hold off the inevitable. He'd never wanted to come more...or less. Daniel wasn't anxious to see this end.

Grasping her wrists, he directed her hands to her breasts. Covering the flesh with her own palms, he held them in place.

"Squeeze," he commanded.

She closed her fingers around her flesh, groaning as she did so. While Sienna pushed at her breasts, he pumped inside her pussy. Her muscles clenched against his. Tighter. So fucking tight.

His grip tensed against her hands, applying even more pressure to her breasts. Her body responded in kind. Her cunt clamping down on him once more.

"Fuck," he said through gritted teeth.

It wasn't enough. It would never be enough. He pulled out, stepped away. Sienna reacted like a scalded cat, her claws coming out to fight.

"No. Don't st—"

He twisted her, lifting her ass to the sink. She winced slightly, and he recalled the spanking. He'd held nothing back and never would again. Sienna would have to learn to deal with that.

He spread her legs and returned, shoving into her pussy while gripping her heated ass in his hands.

Sienna's back arched at his return, her hands clutching his shoulders with a painful, beautiful force. He continued to drive inside until they were both trembling, gasping for air.

Sienna reached up, cupping his face. She drew him toward her. They didn't cease the relentless rhythm of his cock pounding into her pussy. He expected her to kiss him and was shocked when she bit his lip instead.

Her gaze dared him to take her to task. He hadn't mistaken her intent. He'd set out to stake a claim tonight. Apparently Sienna was staking one of her own.

It was the catalyst. He couldn't hold back a second longer. His cock throbbed with its release, spray after hot spray of come filling her. Sienna followed his lead, allowing the wave to crash over her as well.

Together they tumbled, tossed in the swirling vortex of emotions—happiness, confusion, fear, impatience. Daniel felt it. He saw it all reflected in Sienna's face.

For several long minutes after, they never moved, never sought to break apart. Daniel's cock softened within her body. Sienna's hands rested on his shoulders, then—as exhaustion set in—they dropped lower until she was clinging lightly to his waist.

He kissed her softly when their hearts finally stopped racing. Kissing her had become as natural as breathing. And just as vital to him.

"I appreciate you breaking your no sex in a public bathroom rule for me," he teased, trying to find some way to lighten the heaviness surrounding him.

She laughed softly. "God, I sounded like such a prude back then, didn't I?"

"You never fooled me. I saw you for who you really are. Even then."

She swallowed and he thought he saw the glint of a tear in her eye.

A ruckus from the dance reached them. Cheering. Then a countdown.

Loud voices yelled, "*Ten, nine, eight...*"

"It's almost the new year," she whispered.

"*Seven, six, five...*"

He nodded, ran his hand through her hair.

"*Four, three, two...*"

"Happy New Year, Daniel."

"*One!*"

"Happy New Year, Sienna."

And then he kissed her, telling her with his lips exactly what his resolution was.

Chapter Eleven

It was mid-morning. Sienna sat in the family room with Vivi and her cousins, trying to digest the doctor's diagnosis. No one was speaking.

Dr. Spencer had called this morning with the results of his tests and the brain imaging. Vivi was suffering from Alzheimer's disease. While Sienna had suspected the problem for months, there was a big difference between thinking something and learning it for sure. According to Dr. Spencer, Vivi's memory was failing unusually fast.

Sienna, Hope, Sterling and Jade had all accompanied her to the appointment last week, as they'd promised. They'd also kept the checkup a secret from their parents at Vivi's request. Her grandmother refused to cause her boys any worry until they knew something for sure.

Well, now they knew. As soon as she heard the words, Sienna called the other girls. The Mothers had gone shopping this morning. Sienna wished her mom were here right now. She'd know exactly what to say, how to make it all better. Sienna had even suggested calling Jody, but Vivi said no. At this moment, there was quite simply nothing she wouldn't give her grandmother.

"Well. I guess that's it." Vivi's voice was surprisingly strong, laced with her matter-of-fact tone.

"We should call my mom," Hope chimed in. "Maybe there are some other tests they can run. Dr. Spencer could be wrong."

Vivi smiled kindly at Hope. "No, darlin', he's not wrong."

"We should still call my mom," Hope insisted.

Sienna suspected Hope's face reflected her own. Surely someone could offer them some bit of hope, and failing that, they just needed comfort. Aunt Lucy's hugs were the best when it came to consoling them when they'd been younger. Her aunt had always known the way to soothe away the pain of a skinned knee or headache. Maybe Lucy would have an answer for this too.

Vivi clasped her hands, allowing her gaze to slowly travel around the room from face to face. It almost felt as if their grandmother was memorizing their eyes, their names, them. "I'm going to ask you to keep my secret a little bit longer."

Jade shook her head. "No. No, Vivi. We can't do that."

"I'm a selfish old woman and I have no right to ask this of you, but I'm still going to. I lost my JD over twenty years ago. I may be struggling with names and forgetting recipes, God knows I'm repeating myself and driving everyone batty, but I remember the year JD died like it happened yesterday."

Sienna sniffled, fighting hard not to cry. She wasn't going to fall apart. If her other cousins could sit here and be strong for Vivi, she would too.

"His cancer robbed him of his freedom, but worse than that, it took away his pride. He had to rely on his sons' strength to carry him, to carry this ranch. They did it without fail, without question. There wasn't anything they wouldn't do for their daddy. I can't ask them to do that for me. They've done that once. Watched a parent wither away. So I'm asking you. You girls have been my blessing and my strength. My pride won't let me grow weaker in my sons' eyes, not yet. That's something I need time to gear up to."

Hope swiped at her eyes. "Vivi. We'll always take care of you."

Vivi smiled. "I appreciate that. I have some things I need to figure out, things to put into place before we spring this on the family. I just need more time."

"What sort of things?" Jade wouldn't give in easily. Sienna knew that. So did Vivi.

"I think you understand what I'm saying, Jade." Vivi's gaze never left Jade's face, the two of them sharing some unspoken secret.

Jade shook her head. "No. You're fine here. This is your home."

"What are you talking about?" Sterling asked.

Jade rose, anger pouring from her. "Vivi's going to try to find a nursing home, somewhere she can tuck herself away so she won't be a burden on us. That's bullshit! We're not doing that."

"I won't even recognize where I am. Besides I'm not proposing I move there tomorrow. I'm just going to look around, figure out my options. There are lots of nice places I can go and a few of them are quite close to here."

Jade shook her head violently. Before she turned away, Sienna caught a glimpse of the sheen of tears in her too-tough cousin's eyes.

It was Sienna's undoing. "I'm a nurse, Vivi. I can take care of you. When the time comes, I'll take a leave of absence from work if need be. I can be here, night and day. Please let me do that for you."

Vivi's face hardened. "No. Absolutely not. Do you think I would wish that on any of you? I won't remember you. I'll stare through you like you never existed. I'll roam the house at night, keeping you up all hours. You'll have to lock down everything for fear I'll take medicine I'm not supposed to or, God forbid, pick up a knife to chop something. I could unintentionally harm you or your brothers, Sienna. Little Doug." Her grandmother's voice broke on his name. "I won't let his last memories of me be this."

Vivi took a deep breath. When she spoke again, the strength and determination had returned. "There are places where people are trained to take care of folks in my condition. I'm going to stay in one of those. My mind is made up on that and it won't be swayed."

Sienna recognized the stubborn glint in her grandmother's eyes. She'd seen it far too many times over the years. "You knew," Sienna whispered. "You knew this was coming."

Vivi nodded. "I've suspected it for a while. Yes."

Sienna wanted to be angry with her grandmother for hiding her suspicions, her fears. But then, Sienna had had the same worries and she hadn't spoken them aloud either.

"I'll help you find a place to stay," Sterling offered.

Jade shot Sterling a look of pure rage, one that suggested her cousin had stabbed them all in the back.

Sterling didn't relent. "She knows how she wants this to end, Jade. She deserves to do it her way. To face this with her dignity intact. If she has to leave to do that, you can be damn sure I'll stand behind her decision."

"We don't need to think about this right now. We have time." The utter desperation in Hope's voice betrayed exactly how frightened she was. But her cousin was right. They did have time. They all needed to take a step back, let things sink in. Their emotions were too close to the surface. One more word and Sterling and Jade would be at each other's throats.

"Hope's right," Sienna said. "We have some time. Nothing's going to be resolved today."

Vivi released a long, tired sigh. "So you'll keep my secret. Just a little longer?"

Sienna glanced at her cousins, then slowly she nodded. From the corner of her eye, she could see the others follow suit.

Vivi smiled. Silence descended once more until Hope spoke at last.

"Vivi, I don't understand..." Hope's face was filled with anguish. Of all Sienna's cousins, Hope had the biggest heart and the softest soul. She'd spent most of their childhood rescuing strays, caring for injured animals, befriending the lonely kids at school. If Hope sensed suffering, she came running. "How can you be so calm in the face of what's coming?"

Vivi lifted her fingers, beckoned for Hope to join her on the couch. "I'll be okay."

Hope took her grandmother's hand. "All your stories..."

Sienna knew what Hope was mourning. Their childhood had been filled with Vivi's stories, her memories of her own childhood, of Compton Pass and their family. Though they were the younger generation, they'd never felt left behind because Vivi shared all her beautiful memories with them.

"They won't be lost, Hope. I'll tell them all to you." Vivi glanced around as she spoke. "You can carry my memories for me. Then they'll never truly be forgotten."

Sienna tried to swallow around the lump that formed in her throat. It was a touching sentiment. Regardless of how many stories Vivi shared with them, Sienna knew there was one thing she'd never forget and that was her grandmother's strength in the face of true adversity. Sienna let the image of Vivi's face as she appeared now chisel itself into her own memory. She was witnessing true grace under pressure. And it was beautiful.

"I'll keep your memories for you, Vivi." Sterling stepped forward, kneeling before their grandmother, placing her hand on top of Hope's and Vivi's.

"Me too." Sienna added her hand to the pile.

Jade still hovered by the window. Despite her cavalier attitude toward most things, Sienna knew Jade loved deeply. And when she hurt...well, no matter how hard Jade was trying to school her features, hide her agony, it was seeping from every pore.

Finally, Jade stepped forward. "I'm in." She placed her hand on top. They were together. A team of memory keepers. Sisters 'til the end.

Jade was the first to break away. "I need to go."

Sienna wasn't surprised by Jade's desire to escape. Jade needed privacy, somewhere quiet to lick her wounds, to regroup.

"I'm working until close at the bar tonight and I was hoping to catch a nap before then." It was a safe, acceptable excuse.

Hope rose as well. "Do you mind giving me a ride into town, Jade? My shift at the store starts in half an hour."

Jade nodded. They both bent to kiss Vivi on the cheek as they said their goodbyes.

Sterling remained on the floor, kneeling in front of their grandmother. "I'm going to go home, Vivi, and start doing some research on facilities. I'll swing by tomorrow to show you what I find."

Vivi smiled, patting Sterling's cheek softly. "That would be very nice of you." Sterling added her own kiss and left.

Only Sienna remained and her words failed her.

"Don't be sad for me, Sienna. I won't stand for it."

"But Vivi—"

"No. I've lived an amazing life surrounded by my children and my grandchildren. I have no regrets. I don't think anyone can ask for more than that."

She recalled her grandmother's wish, her plan to share her memories with them. She needed a distraction and she suspected Vivi did too. More than that, she needed her grandmother's help. Daniel had mentioned once that time had a way of slipping by too fast. It was dizzying when she considered how quickly the clock was spinning these days. She'd dug in her heels to find some way to make it all stop, but the harder she fought, the greater the force of the current, determined to drag her downstream.

Sienna needed Vivi's wisdom now. Since New Year's, things between her and Daniel had drifted back into the comfortable norm they'd shared before Christmas. She went to his RV every night and lost herself in his arms, but they didn't go out on any more dates. She was almost able to convince herself everything was fine.

But there was something unspoken between them. Words that needed to be said. He was clearly holding back out of respect for her.

New Year's Eve, she'd sensed his feelings, realized what he'd been about to say. And she'd stopped him. Fear and panic had welled up so quickly, she thought she'd suffocate on the stuff. She'd asked him not to say it and, perfect damn man that he was, he hadn't.

The worst part was...she'd wanted him to say it. To tell her he loved her, to hold her, to promise her forever.

But that desire was wrong. Wasn't it? God. She'd known Daniel exactly three months. How could she be so willing to toss away everything she'd ever thought she wanted to take a chance on something so new, so undefined?

She needed help. She needed Vivi's memories before they were lost to her forever.

"Whatever happened to Charles?"

Vivi smiled. "I wondered if you were going to ask me about him. He married a gal from our hometown about a year after I married JD. They had two daughters together. His wife, Joanna, died about six years ago and Charles passed just last year."

"Do you ever wonder what your life would have been like if you'd stayed with him?"

Vivi shook her head. "Life's too short for what-ifs. If it's a rich, full life you're looking for, the best thing you can do is to keep moving forward."

"Yeah, but you got lucky. You found Granddaddy JD."

Vivi snorted and waved her hand. "Shoot, darlin', do you really think I was one-hundred percent sure I was making the right decision when I accepted JD's marriage proposal?"

Sienna reared back, surprised. "You weren't? But you were both so much in love."

"I venture to guess there's not a married woman on the planet who doesn't second-guess herself at least once prior to her wedding day."

Sienna was sure that was true. Although, there was a part of her that had truly believed Vivi and JD were the exception. "So what made you choose JD? How did you know he was the one and not Charles? I mean, it sounds like Charles was a pretty reliable guy too. He and Joanna hung in there for a long time."

"Charles was a wonderful man. I'd never say otherwise. He just wasn't *my* wonderful man."

Sienna's frustration wasn't appeased by her grandmother's

answers. "But how did you *know* that?"

Vivi clasped her hand tightly. "I just did. When JD gazed at me, he saw me. Not just my hair or my face or my body. He saw *me*. And he loved me for who I was, warts and all."

Sienna nodded, her mind whirling. "So you just felt it. Right away?"

Vivi shook her head. "It took a little convincing on JD's part. Like I said, stubbornness runs strong through these veins. What touched my heart was that he kept coming back. No matter how many times I turned him away, he just kept knocking on my door. He made me feel special and needed. While Charles was a kind man, I didn't seem to be vital to his happiness. I could tell he'd be okay with or without me. JD used to tell me I was his heartbeat. He swore he never lived a day until he met me. You'll find your love, Sienna. You'll become his heart. And he'll become yours."

Sienna longed for that kind of love. She'd wasted years of her life, swearing she was happy when all she really felt was fear. Of being alone, of never finding the true love that Vivi shared with JD, that her dad felt for her mom. She wasn't going to be a coward anymore. "I hope so, Vivi."

Her grandmother patted her hand gently. "I think you may be closer to it than you realize. But that doesn't mean you need to rush headlong into anything. You're young. You have time. Life is nothing if not one long crazy voyage. The trick isn't in charting the course. It's merely to keep moving forward and enjoying the scenery."

Sienna recalled Daniel saying something similar on the first day they met. *It's not the destination. It's the journey.*

Bring on the adventure.

Sienna had spent the rest of the afternoon in the quiet

company of her grandmother. They'd watched a couple of old movies, Vivi's favorites, until suppertime. Daniel had pulled her aside briefly after dinner to see if she was okay. She obviously hadn't done a very good job hiding her sadness. She'd assured him they'd talk about it later and he'd accepted her answer.

He was waiting in his usual place when she emerged at midnight. Rather than grasping her hand and dragging her to his RV, he simply opened his arms. She fell into them, soaking up the warmth and comfort of his embrace.

After a few minutes, he whispered in her ear. "Ready?"

She nodded. The walk to his trailer was made in silence. Daniel wouldn't prod her for answers if she wasn't ready to give them. While she'd promised her grandmother she wouldn't share her secret with the family, she couldn't make that same vow in regard to Daniel. She needed someone to talk to, someone who—unlike her cousins—wouldn't be weighted down by emotions that clouded their judgment.

They entered the RV and Daniel helped her take off her coat. "How about we sit for a while? I could make us some hot tea or pour a couple of bourbon and Cokes."

"I don't need anything to drink. I just—" For most of the afternoon she had been able to keep her emotions in check, but when she saw the compassion in Daniel's eyes, the dam broke.

"Hey," he said, reaching for her as the tears started to flow. "Come on now. It can't be that bad." He led her to the couch. Sitting first, he tugged her onto his lap, cuddling her in his embrace. She buried her head in the crook of his neck and simply let it all go.

Daniel's arms tightened around her and she let his strength seep into her bones. She wasn't tough enough to carry this heavy weight alone. He didn't ask what was wrong. Instead, he rocked her gently, rubbed her back, whispering words of comfort.

When the tears began to subside, he cupped her cheek and lifted her gaze until it met his. "Ready to talk about it?"

She nodded. And then she explained. About Vivi's illness, the prognosis. About her grandmother's desire to keep it a secret from the family, her plans to share her memories with the girls and her wish to move into a nursing home. Through it all, Daniel listened, offering her the words she needed to hear.

He thought they were right to keep Vivi's secret. Of all her grandmother's requests, that was the one that sat most heavily upon her shoulders. Daniel convinced her there was no harm in honoring her wishes for the time being. The diagnosis would be the same regardless of when the rest of the family found out. Daniel could sympathize with Vivi's determination to sort out her own affairs before that happened.

He pointed out it how hard it would be for Seth and his brothers to let Vivi go, so she'd have to ease them into that eventuality. Daniel was right. Sienna could picture the fuss Silas would kick up, imagine her father and Sawyer barring the door while Sam promised every penny he'd ever made to any doctor who could offer a cure. Vivi would need the time to prepare herself for that.

Sienna had no doubt her grandmother would win in the end. It reminded her of something Vivi had said back in the fall—Seth would move heaven and earth to keep Jody happy. The same was true for his mother. If Vivi needed to go away to deal with her illness, he might not like it, but eventually, he would resign himself to that end and he would let her go.

"Feeling better?" Daniel reached toward the table for the box of tissues. He grabbed a couple, using them to wipe her eyes, then held them in front of her nose and told her to "Blow."

She laughed, but she blew her nose just the same.

"Daniel," she said, "I don't think I could have gotten through this without you. My cousins—"

"Are as upset as you."

She nodded. "Jade's pissed, Hope's devastated and I can't tell if Sterling is in shock or denial."

"You all have your grandmother's strength. You'll be fine. I promise."

It was exactly what she needed to hear. Sienna leaned forward and kissed him. It wasn't a gentle kiss, rather it was one that was full of demand. And promise.

Daniel hesitated at first. He wouldn't push her or take advantage when she was so distressed. He needn't have worried.

She tackled the buttons on his shirt with haste, desperate to touch his warm skin. She was cold right now. So damn frozen. She needed the heat that only he could provide.

Sienna deepened the kiss, opened her lips to thrust her tongue into Daniel's mouth. He met her halfway. Gripping the hem of her sweater, he drew it over her head.

"Let's go to bed." She rose but remained bent at the waist until he joined her. She refused to give up the solace his mouth provided for even a second. They stumbled to the bedroom together, a mass of limbs trying to walk and undress while their lips never parted.

By the time they reached the bed, they were naked and ravenous. Sienna sat on the edge, dragging Daniel over her as she lay down. Their tongues continued to tangle as Daniel caged her beneath him.

After several minutes of nothing more than soul-stealing kisses, Daniel moved back. "Sienna, if you—"

"Shh." She placed her finger against his lip. "Don't you dare stop now. I need you, Daniel. I need to feel warm again. To feel alive, real, special."

Daniel ran the backs of his fingers along her cheek in a way that made her tremble at the sweetness of the touch. "You are alive, See. And you're the most extraordinary woman I've ever met."

Sienna became aware of her suddenly racing heart. While she was certain it was her arousal that made it pound so furiously, she couldn't help but wonder if her heart had ever truly beat before she met him.

"Make love to me," she whispered.

"Always," Daniel replied.

When they kissed again, the urgency had given way to something much calmer, but no less potent. Sienna opened her legs to welcome him inside and Daniel pressed in slowly.

There was no need to rush. They were starting this journey together.

And they had all the time in the world.

Chapter Twelve

Sienna sighed contentedly against Daniel's chest. She woke up slowly, exhausted. Life was one long, winding road. While she knew Vivi was right, that she needed to keep walking, it was difficult not to miss and mourn the ones who took a different path or who quit walking altogether. She couldn't help but grieve for Vivi, JD, even Charles.

She and Daniel had made love until the wee hours, their motions slow, sensuous and beautiful. She'd tried to tell him she loved him, but the feelings were too new, too fresh. They simply wouldn't come. So instead she'd shown him with her kisses, her caresses.

She lazily opened her eyes, realizing the trailer was too bright. Lifting her head, she glanced at the clock by the side of the bed.

"Shit." She started to rise, but Daniel's arm tightened.

"Stay a few more minutes," he mumbled, still half asleep.

"Daniel. Wake up. It's late. My family will be getting up soon. If they haven't already."

His eyes opened, taking in her panicked state. "We overslept."

Leave it to Daniel to state the obvious. "No shit, Sherlock. I have to get back." She tried once more to rise, but Daniel's grip became viselike around her shoulders. Then he lifted the sheet over her, covering her more completely.

"What are you doing? I don't have time for this. I have to go."

"No. You don't." Daniel's tone was off, strange.

"Why not?"

"Because your family is already awake." Her dad's deep voice filled the small space. Sienna twisted, her gaze taking in what Daniel had already seen, landing on her father filling the doorway to the bedroom.

"Shit," she whispered.

She tugged the sheet higher, but there was no denying she was naked in Daniel's bed.

"Put some clothes on," Dad said. "I'll be waiting for both of you at the house." He turned to leave, but then faced them once more, raising a finger. "Ten minutes," he added. "Be there in ten minutes."

Sienna wasn't sure whether to laugh or cry. Did her dad really think she and Daniel would lounge around in bed and have a quickie?

The door to the RV banged closed, marking her father's departure.

"Guess that's what I get for not locking my door at night."

Sienna tried not to smile at Daniel's jest. Her dad was pissed. She could tell. But, for some reason, it didn't matter. She didn't care. "You realize he's going to rake us over the coals. I'm afraid the next hour or two aren't going to be pleasant."

"Jesus," Daniel said, rising and throwing on yesterday's jeans. "You think he'll rail at us for two hours?"

She lifted one shoulder. "Who knows? I've never actually

gotten caught having sex before."

"You mean to tell me in six years you and Josh never—"

"We were very discreet. And quick. And, well, let's just say you and I have probably had more sex in the past three months than Josh and I usually did in a year."

"Jackass," he muttered.

Sienna giggled, perfectly used to Daniel's opinion of Josh. She was starting to share it. "It'll be fine. We're both adults and there's no way in hell I'll let him fire you for this. I'll recruit my mom and Vivi if I have to. We'll make him understand."

Daniel sat on the edge of the bed, pulling on his boots. "We're consenting adults. Besides I don't give a shit if he does fire me. I'm not leaving Compton Pass, Sienna. I'm not leaving you."

Ever since New Year's, Daniel had worked hard to stake a claim on her heart, but the fact was, he'd owned it for weeks. It was her head that was still waging the battle. No, she was wrong. Even that part of her was finished fighting.

She was in love with Daniel Lennon and, despite her best efforts to remain spontaneous and carefree, her true nature was reappearing—with a vengeance. Plans for the future, their future, were filling up all the cold, lonely spots inside her. She'd never felt so warm.

"You ready?" he asked, reaching out for her.

She nodded and took his hand.

They broke tradition as they returned to her house. Usually, he waited as she snuck in the back door before dawn. Today, they were entering by the front door in broad daylight together.

Doug was standing in the hallway as they entered. His eyes

widened when he caught sight of them, both wearing yesterday's crumpled clothes, their hair messy from sleep.

"Whoa. No wonder Dad's so mad."

"Where is he, Doug?" she asked.

Doug jerked his head to the left, toward the family room. His initial astonishment gave way to concern. "He's not going to fire you, is he, Daniel?"

"I hope not, kiddo."

Doug's shoulders sagged. "Do you think it would help if I went in with you? I can put in a good word."

Daniel walked over to place a friendly hand on her brother's shoulder.

Sienna smiled at the kind gesture, the genuine affection between the boy and the man. She wasn't the only one who'd found a shoulder to cry on, a friend she could rely on. Daniel had offered those same things to Doug in the few months he'd been here.

"I appreciate the offer. Let me see how things go. If I need your help, I'll come find you. Okay?"

Doug nodded. "I'll just be in the stable." He walked out slowly, giving them an encouraging, though somewhat worried, glance over his shoulder as he left.

"Come on." Daniel took her hand once more.

Dad was leaning against his desk, his finger tapping a vicious rhythm out on the cherry wood top. He glanced up when they entered and acknowledged their linked hands with a grimace.

"Have a seat." Dad gestured to the couch.

"Seth—" Daniel started.

"I'm going to speak my piece first, Daniel, so you may as well sit down."

While her dad's tone wasn't exactly friendly, it didn't seem nearly as menacing as it had in the trailer earlier.

She and Daniel sat together. If she'd expected Daniel to try to put a respectable space between them, she really should have known better. They were side by side, their legs touching from hip to knee. She appreciated Daniel's unspoken support. They were in this together.

Dad walked over and claimed the chair across from them. He sank down slowly, releasing a long breath as he did so. "Why didn't you tell me the two of you were involved?"

Sienna had expected a lecture that would take a strip out of her hide. Her father's almost hurt question pierced more. "I was afraid you'd fire Daniel."

Her father nodded, his brows furrowed. "Have I ever been that unreasonable?"

No. He hadn't. The second Dad said the words, Sienna was overcome with guilt. "God, no. It wasn't that. Not really. I was worried about what you'd think of me."

This answer, though more truthful, was worse than the first.

"You're twenty-two years old, Sienna. Do you think I don't realize you have sex? Jesus, your mother took you to the doctor to put you on birth control at seventeen. You don't seriously think I believed that line about it making your periods better, do you?"

She flushed, then grinned. "You're pretty overprotective. You've got to give me that, at least. And you talk a damn good game. Poor Josh didn't touch me for six months after that lecture you gave him about me being your little angel and how you'd do anything to keep me safe. Then you bragged about your days as an amateur boxer. You've never boxed a day in your life."

Daniel chuckled. "Damn. He just told me at Christmas he'd like to see you remain young and innocent for a little while longer."

Sienna turned her attention to Daniel. "He warned you away from me?" Her gaze flew back to her father. "Innocent? You used the word innocent?"

Dad shrugged. "I think I said inexperienced, actually."

Sienna winced. "That's even worse."

"I had to say something. You'd been sneaking out to meet the man for weeks."

Sienna leaned back, her jaw dropping. "You knew? You knew the whole time?"

Dad nodded. "It's an old house with squeaky hardwood floors and your bedroom's right above mine and your mother's. We didn't put you there by accident. Learned that trick from JD when he and Mom stayed in the downstairs bedroom."

Sienna laughed. "God. I love you, Dad."

Her father grinned. "I love you too. You're an adult. I understand that. But that doesn't mean you're not my little girl. You'll always be that."

She recalled Vivi's habit of calling her grown sons *boys*. Though her dad would respect her adult decisions, there was a part of him that would always remember the little girl who crawled onto his lap each night for a bedtime story. And as his child, she'd been too worried about disappointing him to come clean about what had truly begun as a casual affair.

Dad shrugged. "You could have told me about Daniel."

She realized that now. Hell, she'd always known it. "I'm sorry I didn't." She rose from the couch and walked over to her dad. He stood, welcoming her into his strong embrace. Her dad gave some of the world's greatest hugs. The only ones that had ever come close to comparing were Daniel's.

"Now," Dad said. "If you'll excuse us a minute, Sienna, I think Daniel and I need to have a little chat. Man to man."

She shook her head. "Hell no."

Daniel stood. "It's okay, Sienna. Your dad's right."

She glanced at him nervously. "Daniel—"

"Just give us a few minutes," Daniel prodded.

She flashed her father an unspoken warning, not that she expected it to work.

"Don't worry. I'm not going to hurt your boyfriend, Sienna." And then, because he was a horrible tease, Dad added, "Much."

"Fine. I'll just go find Mom and Vivi." She could issue threats as well as her father. If there was any force capable of holding her dad back, it was Seth's wife and his mother. Sienna wasn't completely without backup.

She stopped at the doorway to the hall and glanced back. Daniel gave her a reassuring wink.

With that, she left.

"So what's the plan?"

Daniel frowned at Seth's question. "Plan?"

Seth crossed his arms. "Don't play stupid, Daniel. You got it bad for her. But something tells me she hasn't quite figured that out yet."

Daniel grimaced and sank back onto the couch. "She knows."

"Ah," Seth nodded, reclaiming his own seat. "She still hung up on Josh?"

Daniel shook his head. "No. I don't think so." The more he thought of it, the more he realized Josh really was out of the picture. "No. She's not," he added, more firmly.

"I'm glad to hear it. So what's your next move?"

"God, Seth. I wish I could figure one out. I considered taking a page from your book, but I'm guessing I wouldn't have your blessing to kidnap Sienna and hide her away until she comes around."

"You wouldn't."

Daniel chuckled. "Yeah. I didn't think so. You can blame your brothers for that idea, by the way. They planted a seed at Christmas when they talked about the way you proposed to Jody."

Seth nodded. "So noted. I'll find my brothers after we finish up here and kick their asses instead since I foolishly promised my daughter I wouldn't hurt you. Won't be the first time."

"I love her, Seth. I'm in love with her. I feel like I've been thrown off the bull and now he's crushing my guts out under his hooves."

"That sounds about right."

Daniel looked at Seth incredulously. "Nothing about this feels right. Every time I think I'm getting through to her, every time I feel like maybe she's starting to care for me, she takes three big steps back. Doesn't help that Josh keeps creeping in every now and then. Everyone she loves keeps telling her to get out there, that there are other fish in the sea. She spent years of her life, walking toward a future that was certain in her mind. I've been here less than three months and I'm asking her to throw all that away, to take a chance on me."

"Can I give you a little advice?"

"Hell yeah." Daniel was grateful for the offer. He'd come to respect Seth Compton as much as he did his own father. Seth wouldn't lead him wrong.

"You're not going to like it," Seth warned.

Daniel frowned. "Are you going to tell me to stop seeing Sienna?"

Seth shook his head. "No. Be a waste of breath if I did. Keeping you away from that girl would be as easy as separating Doug from his horse. No, it's just this. You're gonna have to give her time."

Daniel blew out a long breath. "How much time?"

Seth chuckled. "You expect me to give you a date? Doesn't work that way. She just got out of a long-term relationship with an idiot she truly planned to marry. She's still smartin' over that. You two are obviously head over heels in love. Pretty compatible, I'd say."

Daniel couldn't hold back his cocky grin as he considered just how well-suited they were—in the bedroom and out. "We're a good fit. A real good fit."

Seth raised his hand in warning. "I can still kick your ass, son."

Daniel laughed. "Sorry. So you're telling me to slow down. Stop trying to force it."

Seth stood and walked to the fireplace mantel. Daniel spotted a photograph of a much younger Seth and Jody on their wedding day there. Seth ran his finger along the frame almost absentmindedly. "It's not an easy thing. I see a lot of myself in you. When men like us make up our mind about how things are going to be, that's it. We move forward and God help anybody who gets in our way. I made a lot of mistakes when I was trying to win Jody's heart. I pushed her away with both hands for years because she had some growing up to do. Problem was, when I finally reached out for her, she wasn't reaching back."

Daniel nodded. "I let Sienna believe we were having a casual affair. Pretended it was something easy, something she could control. Shame of it is I wasn't just lying to her, I was lying to myself too. I latched on to the no-strings deal because I figured that was enough, all I needed. What if she *never* reaches out for me?"

Seth turned to face him once more. "That's where the time thing comes in. Sienna is questioning her judgment on everything these days. I guess that's not a comfortable place for a girl who's always had her life figured out. All you can do is hang in there. Be the man she needs. Be honest about how you feel. If you're a religious man, a bit of prayer might not hurt."

Daniel sniggered, but he appreciated the advice. "Okay. So the plan stays the same. Take it one day at a time and hope I manage to wear her down."

Seth walked back to his desk and plopped down in the large leather chair with a shit-eating grin on his face. "And if that fails, you resort to plan B."

"What's plan B?"

"We revisit the kidnapping idea."

Chapter Thirteen

Daniel drove the ranch truck one-handed. His other arm was occupied, wrapped around Sienna's shoulder. She'd opted to ride in the middle of the cab. It was Valentine's Day. It was also his first "date" with Sienna since talking to Seth three weeks earlier.

He'd taken Seth's advice and slowed things down, allowing things with Sienna to fall into a normal—God, if he could call Heaven normal—pattern. Neither he nor Sienna had talked about their feelings, and subjects like commitment and the future simply didn't come up.

At least, they hadn't until now. He hoped a romantic atmosphere would soften Sienna, make her more receptive to his affections. He was adding a new word to their relationship vocabulary tonight—love. He loved her and he was going to tell her.

Life had turned into one perfect day after another. He and Sienna would eat with her family every night, then pile into the family room to watch TV or play games. Sienna kept a close eye on Vicky and often the two women stole away for some private time. Her grandmother was determined to share her stories—of childhood, of marriage and of raising children. Sienna had confessed to Vicky that Daniel knew about her diagnosis as well. As a result, he'd been told a few stories himself. Vicky had shared some entertaining memories about crazy things JD had done when he was a younger man to woo her. Daniel appreciated Vicky's matchmaking help and was sorry he'd never met JD.

As evening gave way to night, he and Sienna would walk to his RV together. There was no more hiding or sneaking about. When darkness descended, they came together in a tangle of limbs and lips. Sometimes their lovemaking was a rough, heart-racing ride, wilder than his eight seconds on the bull. Other times it was slow and peaceful as a country ballad. Afterwards, they'd fall asleep in each other's arms. Come morning, he'd leave early, as his chores on the ranch started at first light. Sienna took a bit more time with her waking. She'd return home, shower, dress and head to work. Then he'd spend the entire day watching the clock and waiting for her to return.

He knew what his future should be, but Seth was right—a few months wasn't all that long. Rushing things was only going to push her away.

As they pulled into town, Daniel drove down Main Street, seeking a place to park. He'd made reservations at the fanciest restaurant in town and then told her last night he was taking her out for the holiday. He'd held his breath as he'd waited for her reply, hoping her fear of hopping back into the "dating scene" had abated since New Year's. She'd smiled at the invitation and accepted immediately.

"Wow. Charlotte went all out."

He glanced over to see what had caught Sienna's eye. He fought to restrain a groan. Charlotte, the owner of Northstar Restaurant, had obviously spared no expense on decorating the windows in a sea of red silk and roses.

"Yeah." His soft sigh must have given him away as Sienna giggled.

"Aw, come on, Daniel. You know you love all this mushy-gushy shit. Cupids and hearts with arrows through them and chocolates. Maybe Charlotte's hired Janine from the local high school to stroll around the place playing the violin again."

Daniel parked the truck on the side of the street, then glanced at Sienna. "Please tell me you're joking about the violin."

Sienna's grin grew. "Sorry. Can't do that. She's had a year to practice, so I'm sure she's better than last year."

"Were you here last year?"

Sienna shook her head. "No. I was away at school. Hope told me about it. It was really sweet of you to go to all this trouble. I understand that Valentine's Day isn't exactly a guy holiday."

Daniel considered contradicting her. There were parts of this day that were definitely for him. In addition to the flowers he'd given her when he picked her up for their date, there was still a wrapped package on his bed that contained the sexiest red teddy he'd ever seen and pair of furred-lined handcuffs.

Oh, he fully intended to enjoy the holiday. Unfortunately, the fun stuff apparently wasn't going to start until he'd spent the next two hours listening to some girl named Janine butcher "Lady of Spain".

Daniel climbed out of the truck, crossing to open Sienna's door for her. She was wearing a hot pink dress with a v-neck that showed off her cleavage a bit too well for his peace of mind. He'd had to make several adjustments to his pants since first seeing her and he'd even tried to make a deal with his cock. *Go away through dinner and reap the rewards all night long.* Damn thing had a head of its own. Literally. It wasn't going anywhere.

She stepped out of the vehicle, keeping her hand in his as he led her to the restaurant. The inside of the restaurant was designed with lovers in mind. Each table was covered in a long white tablecloth with a single red rose lying across the lady's plate. The lighting was dim enough to allow the flickering candles to complete the ambiance. So far, so good. There was no teenaged strolling violinist. Instead there was the soft sound of piano music filling the air.

It was perfect.

The hostess led them to a small table in the middle of the floor. Sienna picked up her rose and smelled it. "This is all so nice."

Charlotte really had outdone herself. They'd arrived earlier than most of the dinner crowd. Daniel had purposely chosen the first seating offered since he intended to spend the majority of the night in bed with Sienna. As a result, only about half of the tables were full. He was glad. It added to the magic of the evening. They could pretend they were the only two people in the place.

The waitress came over to take their drink orders and since they were doing an abbreviated menu for the special occasion, she asked them for their dinner preferences. Daniel opted for the steak, while Sienna ordered the vegetarian lasagna.

Daniel reached across the table, clasping her hand in his. "You look beautiful in candlelight. Remind me to get some candles for the RV."

She leaned forward, the new position giving him far too nice a view of her breasts as they peeked out from beneath her dress. "Thank you for inviting me out tonight, Daniel."

He shrugged. "It's a holiday for lovers."

Her fingers tightened around his and, for a moment, he got a sense that she was going to say something. Her face was serious, pensive. Unfortunately, the expression morphed to one of surprise.

"Josh?"

He frowned when Sienna dropped his hand and straightened.

"What?" he asked.

Sienna didn't reply. Instead, her gaze focused on someone coming in the restaurant. Daniel gritted his teeth as he watched Josh making his way over to their table. Fuck.

Josh walked right up to Sienna, his eyes failing to take in the fact that Daniel was at the table. "Sienna. I thought that was you. I was across the street at my parents' store when I spotted you."

Sienna must have noticed that Josh had failed to acknowledge his presence as well. She gestured toward Daniel. "Josh, you remember Daniel, don't you?"

Daniel stood. "We met at Thanksgiving."

Josh nodded absentmindedly as they shook hands. Daniel resisted the urge to squeeze the man's fingers tightly as a warning. "Oh, sure. Yeah. I remember."

"What are you doing here?" Sienna asked. "Why aren't you at school?"

Josh turned back to Sienna and stepped closer to her. Daniel's shoulders tensed and he took a steadying breath. It didn't appear to have sunk into Josh's thick skull that Daniel and Sienna were on a date.

"I hopped in the car right after lunch and drove four hours to get here," Josh explained.

Sienna seemed genuinely perplexed. "Why?"

"To see you." Josh's face was the picture of earnestness. Daniel closed his eyes briefly to block out the image. Josh had finally figured it out. Realized what he'd let go.

Sienna didn't appear pleased by Josh's appearance. "Josh.

I don't think—"

"I screwed up." Josh cut her off. Sienna raised her hand, but he kept talking. "I'm sorry, See. I've been so miserable without you."

"Josh, stop." Sienna tried to halt the man's onslaught of words, but they continued to flow, growing more desperate with each passing moment. "I love you so much. I always have. I was wrong when I said I didn't know who I was."

Sienna shook her head. "No. You weren't wrong. We were so young when we started dating."

Several of the diners at nearby tables began watching the drama unfolding. Daniel wasn't sure how to stop what was happening. He wasn't sure he should, so instead he dropped back into his seat and held his tongue.

Josh grasped her hand. "You always said we were lucky because we met when we were young. These past few months without you have been so hard for me."

Tears began to form in Sienna's eyes. Daniel swallowed hard. *Jesus. What if Sienna felt the same?*

"We needed the time apart, Josh. I said I knew who I was, but I didn't. I do now."

Daniel studied her face, hope warring with fear. Sienna never glanced Daniel's way, her gaze holding steadfast on Josh.

Then Josh knelt, sucking all the air out of the room. A woman at the table next to them gasped softly.

No, Daniel thought. *No.* He didn't need to speak the word. Sienna did.

"No." Panic covered her features. "Oh my God, no. Josh, stand up."

Josh didn't hear the warning, didn't understand. "I love

you, Sienna Compton. I've loved you since I was fifteen years old."

"Don't do this." Sienna spoke quietly. "Stop. Stop right now. Please." Her voice broke on the last word, but Josh was a man on a mission. No force of nature was going to prevent this proposal.

Sienna shook her head, but Josh forged on. "It's just like you've always said. We'll spend the rest of our lives with each other, grow old together."

Sienna sucked in a painful gasp when Josh produced a ring from his pocket. "Shit," she breathed.

"I stopped by my parents' house first. This ring belonged to my grandmother. I was on my way to Compass Ranch when I saw you. Sienna Compton, will you marry me?"

The question hovered in the air. The restaurant had gone silent, every eye in the place on the odd tableau they created. Daniel and Sienna seated at the table. Josh on his knees holding out a ring.

Daniel wasn't sure how much time passed. To him, it felt like a millennium as he waited for the response that could destroy him.

Sienna froze, her mind struggling to process what was going on. As she glanced around the room, she could tell every person there was waiting for her answer.

God. How long had she been sitting here? A year? A minute? Had her heart beat once? Twice? She had to speak.

"No." Sienna shook her head. It brought her no joy to hurt her first love, but she wouldn't lie to Josh. Wouldn't pretend anymore. "I won't marry you, Josh."

Josh's face reflected a myriad of emotions, each of them

passing quickly. Confusion, denial, anger, sadness. "I said I was sorry. I was wrong. Really wrong. Please forgive me, take me back."

He truly thought the past few months could be put away so easily?

She hated hurting him. God, she despised what she was doing right now, but it simply couldn't be helped. "Stand up, Josh," she whispered.

The waitress came back with their drinks and softly asked if they'd like another chair.

Daniel nodded.

She brought one and Josh sank into it heavily. "Tell me what to do to make the last few months up to you, See. I'll do anything."

It was so like Josh to look to her for the answer. Then she remembered something Vivi said. "You are a wonderful man, Josh. You're just not *my* wonderful man."

She glanced at Daniel and saw him blink with surprise when she smiled at him.

For the first time since he entered the restaurant, Josh seemed to really take notice of Daniel. "You and Daniel?"

She nodded, then licked her lips nervously as she held Daniel's gaze. "I'm in love with him."

Daniel didn't move, didn't respond. He didn't have to. His eyes said it all. She'd never been gazed at with such compassion, adoration...love.

Josh glanced from her to Daniel and back again. "But you barely know each other."

"My heart recognizes him."

Daniel smiled, gave her a charming wink, then he turned his attention to Josh. "Listen, Josh. This probably doesn't help, but I'm in love with Sienna and I intend to spend the rest of my life making her happy."

Josh rose slowly. "You're right, Daniel. It doesn't help. But I'm glad to hear it just the same."

He turned back to Sienna. She had to fight the tears building. She'd never felt so completely torn. How could one person be utterly overjoyed and completely devastated at the same time? Josh was the first boy she'd ever loved and she was breaking his heart. But Daniel sat next to her, his quiet strength filling her with happiness and peace.

Josh shrugged ruefully, the boyish gesture reminding her of when they were younger. "I am sorry, Sienna."

She nodded, batting away a tear as it fell. "I'm sorry too."

Josh left as Sienna tried to get herself together. She used her napkin to dry her eyes.

Daniel didn't say anything. Instead, he raised his hand for the waitress. He quietly asked if they could get their food to go. The woman nodded and returned to the kitchen.

He reached over and took her hand. "You okay?"

"I guess so. I didn't like hurting him."

"I know. You tried to stop him, See. He was determined to issue that proposal. I don't blame him. If I thought you were slipping away from me, I'd fight like the devil to drag you back."

She smiled sadly at his admission, then she repeated the words she'd longed to say for weeks. "I love you."

He lifted her hand and kissed it. "I love you too."

"I have a new life plan."

He chuckled. "Okay. Let's hear it."

"I'll warn you now. It's pretty intense. Downright complicated."

His brow creased, concern touching his gaze. Even so, he didn't move away. "What do you want?"

"To be happy."

"That's it?" he asked.

"You know, that's not as simple as you might think. How would you feel about spending the next few months with me as your girlfriend? I thought maybe we could take some time to get to know each other while going with the flow?"

He pretended to consider her request, tapping his chin as if in deep thought. She wasn't worried. She could see mischief brewing.

"We still get to have sex, right?"

She laughed. "Absolutely."

"Then I think that plan sounds real nice."

The waitress brought their doggie bag. Daniel handed her enough money for the meal and the tip, then took the food. Rising, he grasped Sienna's hand and together they walked to the truck.

Once they were both inside, Daniel turned to her. "Sienna. Just so you know, my new life plan's a lot simpler than yours."

"It is?"

He nodded. "Yep. I'm going to spend the rest of my life with you."

The rest of their ride back to the ranch was made in silence. Too many things had happened in a matter of minutes. Sienna was grateful to Daniel for giving her space to sort through it all. By the time they reached his RV, she felt calmer, more together.

Daniel led her inside. "We could hang out for a little while. Talk."

She shook her head. Reaching for the hem of her dress, she

pulled the entire thing over her head in one fast swoop. Daniel's gaze drifted slowly over her matching bra and panty set. They were hot pink like her dress. She'd bought the entire ensemble after recalling Daniel's confession once that he got turned on by the sight of her in hot pink nursing scrubs.

"Dayum." Daniel's twang made her laugh...and made her hot. He stepped closer, reaching behind her to unhook her bra. "As much as I like the look of this, I don't want anything between us tonight."

She slipped her panties down as he stripped the lacy bra away. Bending at the waist, he took one of her nipples in his mouth, sucking hard. Sienna's hands flew to his head, holding him close. She marveled at his ability to make her feel treasured and horny as hell at the same time.

He moved to the other breast, his hands and lips working their magic. Sienna felt the effects of his attention clear to her toes.

She loved him. Why had she fought those words, that truth for so long?

Sienna pushed him away. Daniel took a step back, surprised to be stopped until she dropped to her knees and began to tackle the fastening on his pants.

"Oh hell yeah," he murmured, his hands tangling in her hair when she released his cock and took the head into her mouth.

She'd never felt so ravenous, so hungry. There was nothing she wouldn't give this man. He'd found her when she was at a low point in her life. With his strong hands and sturdy back, he helped her up, even carried her a few times until she was ready to stand on her own two feet again, ready to take on the world.

Daniel shrugged off his pants carefully as she continued to suck him. As she gripped the base of his cock, he pulled his shirt over his head. It was always this way. After months, they still came together every night as if it was the first time.

His cock brushed the back of her throat and his hands flew to her head as he groaned. "God, Sienna. You're so fucking amazing."

She moved faster at his praise, taking him deeper. Reaching lower, she cupped his balls with her free hand. Daniel jerked like he'd touched an electric wire, slipping from her mouth.

"Daniel—" She started to complain when his hands grasped hers, pulling her up.

"No. Not this way." He twisted her, propelled her toward the bedroom. She started to protest, determined to finish.

"On the bed," he demanded.

"But—"

He kissed her suddenly, a hard, fast buss. Then he cupped her cheek, forced her gaze to his. "Trust me."

She crawled onto the bed and spotted a wrapped packaged. Daniel pushed it aside. "Later. I promise."

She grinned, enjoying his haste, his impatience. She lay down, expecting him to crawl over her, to come inside. She even parted her legs, ready for him.

"Nope. Not yet." He twisted until his hips were even with her head, his shoulders between her legs.

"Oh yeah," she whispered when his lips lightly grazed her clit. Covering her, upside down, Daniel wasted no time running his tongue along her wet slit.

She hissed at the sensation, then gripped his cock.

Daniel groaned when she took him deep on the first pass. He countered the motion, nipping at her clit, then teasing it with his talented tongue.

Sienna struggled for air, his touches taking her too far. She increased the suction on his cock and was rewarded with Daniel's revenge when he thrust his tongue inside her pussy.

Soon it became an all-out battle of wills as each of them tried to drive the other to the peak. The trick for Sienna was not falling over the top herself. When Daniel added a finger to the play, teasing the rim of her anus, she fought for control.

Then she got even. *Tit for tat*, she thought, as she sucked one of her fingers into her mouth alongside Daniel's cock. She didn't give him long to wonder what she was doing when she pushed the wet digit into his ass, straight to the second knuckle.

Daniel bucked roughly, dislodging her finger. She started to go in for a second pass, but he cut her off, flipping around on the bed.

"Bad girl," he said, though his glazed eyes told her he was far from disgusted with her play. In fact, his gaze was downright encouraging. They'd definitely be exploring that territory again.

But Daniel clearly had different plans tonight and his sense of fair play was thrown out the window when he knelt between her legs and pushed his tongue against her clit once more.

"No fair," she gasped.

Daniel didn't bother to respond. Instead he proved to her just how unfair he could be. Pushing two fingers inside her pussy, he finger-fucked her until she lost track of her surroundings, her name, the whole lot...everything just disappeared. Her hips rose to meet him. When she finally came, it hit her like a tidal wave, kicking her feet out from under her and tossing her like a rag doll through the crashing water.

She'd thought the climax was amazing. She was wrong.

Daniel came over her as she yelled out her release, his cock slamming in to the hilt as she still drifted amongst the wreckage. His rough entry triggered another spasm and lightning flashed behind her closed eyelids.

He offered no reprieve. Instead, he gave her everything he had and, as her body continued to tremble, it felt like more than she could handle.

Her loud cries gave way to hoarse moans and still Daniel thrust inside her, ruthlessly. She ran her fingernails down his arms, clawing her way closer.

"Too good," she said, gasping for breath. "It's too much."

Daniel kissed her roughly, and then shook his head. "Never."

As she cried out for mercy, her body continued to beg for more. He was right. A lifetime wouldn't be enough. He'd spoken the word written on her heart. Never. She'd never tire of him, never get enough, never stop loving him. Never.

Sienna came again, the orgasm taking her by surprise, shaking her until her teeth chattered. And still Daniel moved.

She didn't resist, didn't fight the onslaught. She was finished with denials, with lies.

"Mine," she whispered.

"Always."

She wasn't sure if he was waiting for the word or if his body had finally reached its limit, but Daniel came.

She watched his face in silent wonder as his climax began to wane. He fell next to her in a heap. His eyes remained closed, his face more peaceful than she'd ever seen it.

Vivi had been right.

He was her heart.

And she was his.

Epilogue

"Remember your sixteenth birthday?"

Sienna glanced at Hope, wondering why on earth her cousin was thinking of that after all these years. Spring was making an early appearance. The icy cold winter had thawed early this year, Mother Nature turning on the heat in March rather than waiting for April. She and Hope were taking advantage of the sunshine, sitting in the back garden.

Vivi was worried about the fact her bulbs were blooming early. She was certain a cold spell would come and ruin her colorful spring garden.

Sienna sighed. "Hell yeah I remember. We all got in big trouble. Jake still likes to tease me about the time he and Dad had to carry four giggling, drunk-ass girls down from the hayloft."

Hope giggled. "My head ached for days after."

"What made you think of that?"

Her cousin shrugged. "I don't know. Life just seemed a lot simpler at sixteen."

Sienna nodded. "You can say that again. I was so sure of myself back then. Had my whole future figured out."

"Then Daniel showed up."

Sienna grinned. "And tossed everything I thought I wanted

out on its ear."

"I don't think I ever realized it before, but I've never seen you in love. Not really. I like the way it looks on you."

Sienna wondered if she should contradict her cousin. She had loved Josh. Truly loved him, but maybe it was semantics. Given the way she felt about Daniel, she could understand the difference between loving someone and being in love. It seemed like a short distance separated the two. In reality, they were as close as California and New York.

Hope was quiet for a few moments. Sienna noticed the sadness that had taken up residence in her cousin's eyes for weeks creep in again. "What's wrong, Hope? Are you still worried about Vivi?"

Hope nodded. "Yeah. Of course. But I don't see that feeling going away anytime soon."

"It's more than that. Isn't it?"

Hope sighed, rubbing her eyes wearily. "I still wish for what I wanted at sixteen. But I'm afraid maybe it's just a silly girl's dream. Something impossible."

Sienna knew what Hope wanted. While she longed to reassure Hope it wasn't unattainable, she knew the odds were rather slim. Hope had grown up in an unconventional home, but one that worked. Uncle Silas, Uncle Colby and Aunt Lucy were meant to be together. While their love was different, it didn't make the union any less special, perfect.

She reached out to grasp Hope's hand. "You're beautiful, smart and sweet. I don't doubt for a minute that when you find love, it will be beyond your wildest dreams."

But Hope wanted more from her. Sienna could see it. She needed Sienna's assurance that there might be *two* men out there who would claim her heart and give her the life she desired more than anything.

Offering those words wouldn't be fair. If Sienna had learned anything this winter, it was that what you wanted didn't always match up with what you got. But that didn't make the prize any less sweet, any less magical.

"Hope. I think you're going to have to go with the flow on this one. You can't force it. Love comes where it comes. And we just have to make sure that when it shows up, our heart and our eyes are open enough to see it. To feel it."

Hope smiled, her face clearing. "You're right. I need to shake off these winter blues. The flowers are blooming, the birds are singing. And hope springs eternal."

About the Authors

Jayne Rylon and Mari Carr met at a writing conference in June 2009 and instantly became archenemies. Two authors couldn't be more opposite. Mari, when free of her librarian-by-day alter ego, enjoys a drink or two or...more. Jayne, allergic to alcohol, lost huge sections of her financial-analyst mind to an epic explosion resulting from Mari gloating about her hatred of math. To top it off, they both had works in progress with similar titles and their heroes shared a name. One of them would have to go.

The battle between them for dominance was a bloody, but short one, when they realized they'd be better off combining their forces for good (or smut). With the ink dry on the peace treaty, they emerged as good friends, who have a remarkable amount in common despite their differences, and their writing partnership has flourished. Except for the time Mari attempted to poison Jayne with a bottle of Patrón. Accident or retaliation? You decide.

Jayne and Mari can be found troublemaking on their Yahoo loop at: groups.yahoo.com/group/Heat_Wave_Readers/join

You can follow their book-loving insanity on Twitter or Facebook or send them each a personal note at contact@jaynerylon.com or carmichm1@yahoo.com.

How strong are the ties that bind?

Western Ties
© *2012 Mari Carr & Jayne Rylon*
Compass Brothers, Book 4

Leah Hollister's sex life needs a swift kick in the pants. Small-town Compton Pass, though, isn't the place to explore her need for bondage. When she gets an invitation to a BDSM party out in LA, she wastes no time booking a flight.

Her plan to play anonymously is shot to hell when she runs into high-school crush Sawyer Compton—and he lays immediate claim to her.

Sawyer Compton commands total control, in and out of the bedroom. He never thought Leah could handle his darker urges, but one look at the white bracelet that marks her as a sub ripe for the picking, and he knows exactly how this night is going to end. With Leah in his bed.

Leah didn't expect to enjoy the comfort Sawyer's familiarity brings, even as his touch takes her to unimaginable heights of pleasure. When bad news from home sends him reeling, she's more than prepared to offer him anything he needs: her body, her friendship. Even her heart—if Sawyer can loosen the reins over his own to accept her love.

Warning: Invest in tissues. Lots and lots of tissues. Between spicy, set-the-sheets-on-fire bondage romps and the last Compass brother coming home, you'll need them.

Available now in ebook and print from Samhain Publishing.

He's faced down every demon...
except one fast-talking Southern girl.

Lost in You
© *2013 Lauren Dane*
Petal, Georgia, Book 2

It hasn't been easy for Joe Harris to live down his not-so-honorable past, but the military made him a better man. He's determined to make up for past mistakes, starting with coming home to care for his ailing father.

Things are going as planned until his best friend's little sister comes barreling into his life. Funny, quick talking, smart, beautiful, she's a temptation he tries—and fails—to resist.

When Beth Murphy hears Joe is back in town, she makes sure she's the first on his welcoming committee. Though he tries to pretend he's gruff and unworthy of her, she sees the man who spoils his dog, who touches her like she's precious. Cherished. But there's one wall she can't break down—the truth about what's happening at home.

On the night the nature of his father's illness becomes painfully, publicly apparent, Joe does the right thing—push Beth as far away as possible. But if he thought she'd go away quietly, he's about to learn she's made of sterner stuff.

Warning: Slow-talking, sexy mechanic with a drawl, looking to get a Murphy right out of her underpants. Quick-talking woman who knows what she wants and has a weak spot for the aforementioned slow-talking mechanic and his dancing dog. Bad words. Polly Chase behind the wheel again.

Available now in ebook and print from Samhain Publishing.

SAMHAIN
PUBLISHING

It's all about the story...

Romance

HORROR

Retro ROMANCE

www.samhainpublishing.com

CPSIA information can be obtained at www.ICGtesting.com
Printed in the USA
BVOW05s0349170615
404740BV00002B/4/P